Geronimo Stilton

FOLLOWING THE TRAIL OF MARCO POLO

Geronimo Stilton

GRAPHIC NOVELS AVAILABLE FROM PAPERCUTZ™

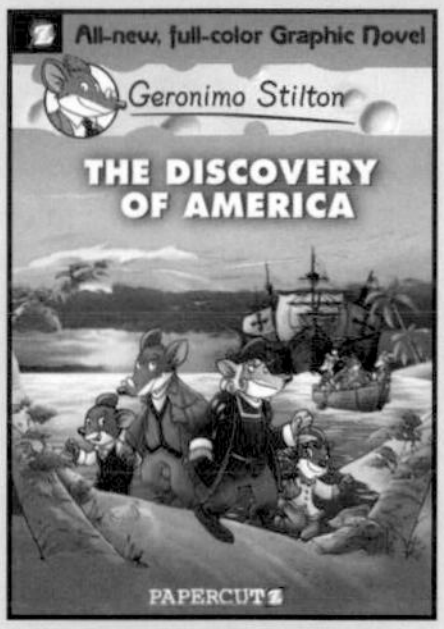
All-new, full-color Graphic Novel
Geronimo Stilton
THE DISCOVERY OF AMERICA
PAPERCUTZ

Graphic Novel #1
"The Discovery of America"

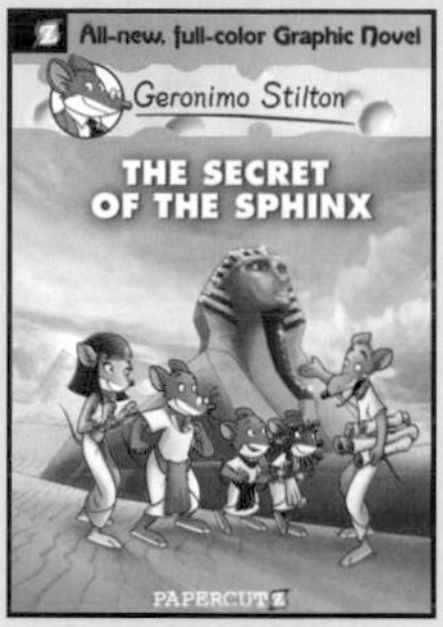
All-new, full-color Graphic Novel
Geronimo Stilton
THE SECRET OF THE SPHINX
PAPERCUTZ

Graphic Novel #2
"The Secret of the Sphinx"

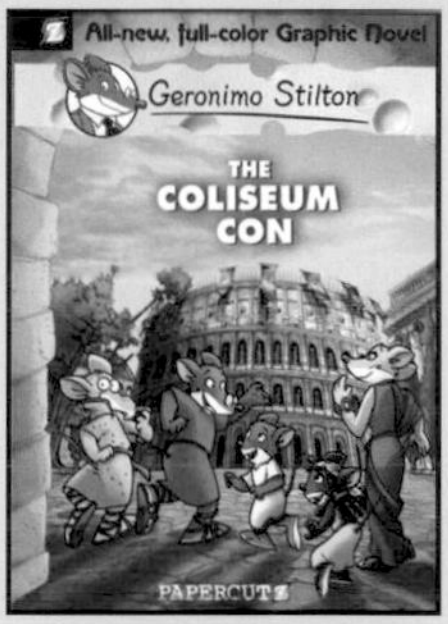
All-new, full-color Graphic Novel
Geronimo Stilton
THE COLISEUM CON
PAPERCUTZ

Graphic Novel #3
"The Coliseum Con"

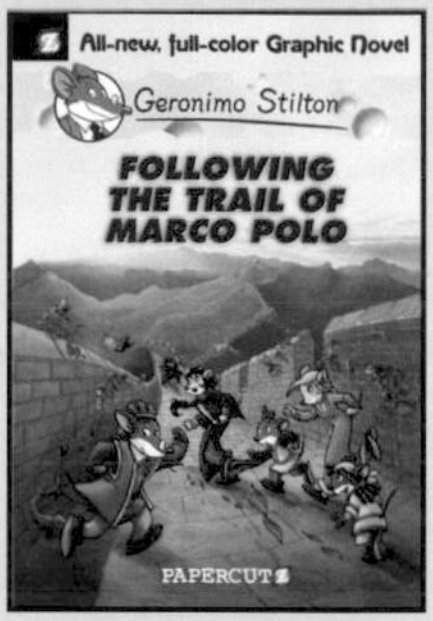
All-new, full-color Graphic Novel
Geronimo Stilton
FOLLOWING THE TRAIL OF MARCO POLO
PAPERCUTZ

Graphic Novel #4
"Following the Trail of Marco Polo"

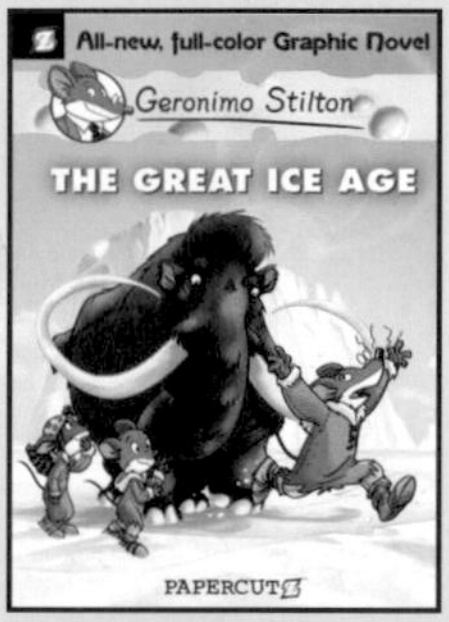
All-new, full-color Graphic Novel
Geronimo Stilton
THE GREAT ICE AGE
PAPERCUTZ

Graphic Novel #5
"The Great Ice Age"

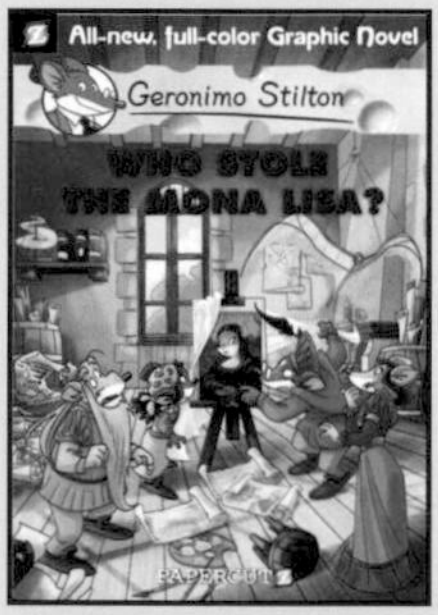
All-new, full-color Graphic Novel
Geronimo Stilton
WHO STOLE THE MONA LISA?
PAPERCUTZ

Graphic Novel #6
"Who Stole The Mona Lisa?"

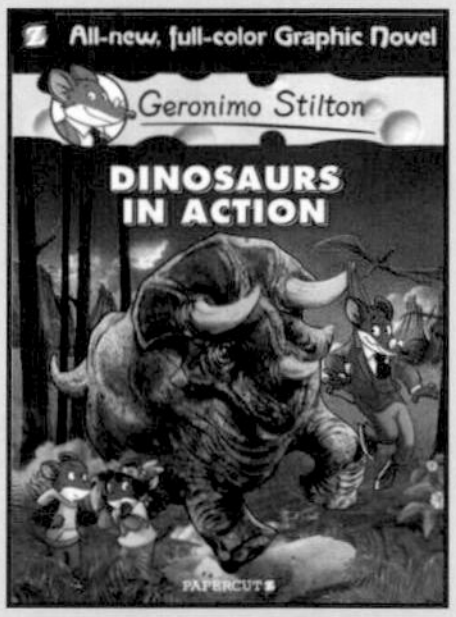
All-new, full-color Graphic Novel
Geronimo Stilton
DINOSAURS IN ACTION

Graphic Novel #7
"Dinosaurs in Action"

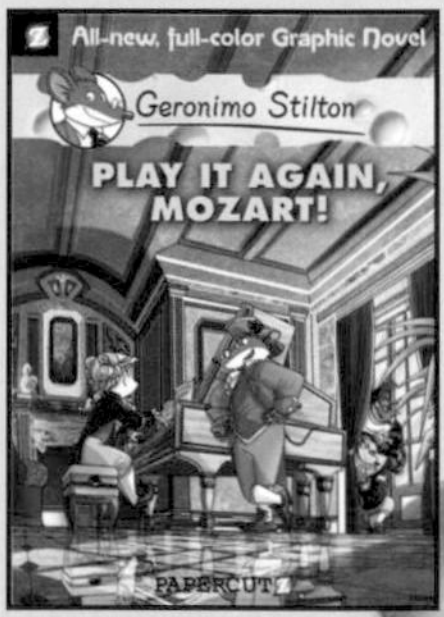
All-new, full-color Graphic Novel
Geronimo Stilton
PLAY IT AGAIN, MOZART!
PAPERCUTZ

Graphic Novel #8
"Play It Again, Mozart!"

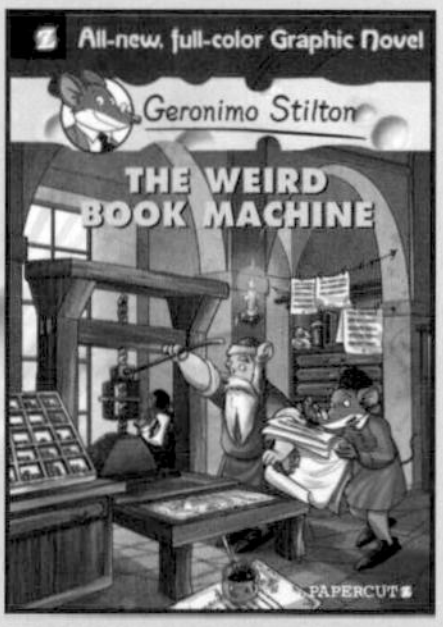
All-new, full-color Graphic Novel
Geronimo Stilton
THE WEIRD BOOK MACHINE
PAPERCUTZ

Graphic Novel #9
"The Weird Book Machine"

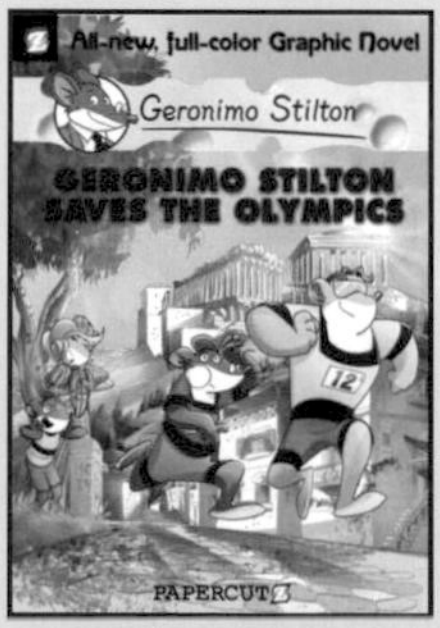
All-new, full-color Graphic Novel
Geronimo Stilton
GERONIMO STILTON SAVES THE OLYMPICS
PAPERCUTZ

Graphic Novel #10
"Geronimo Stilton Saves the Olympics"

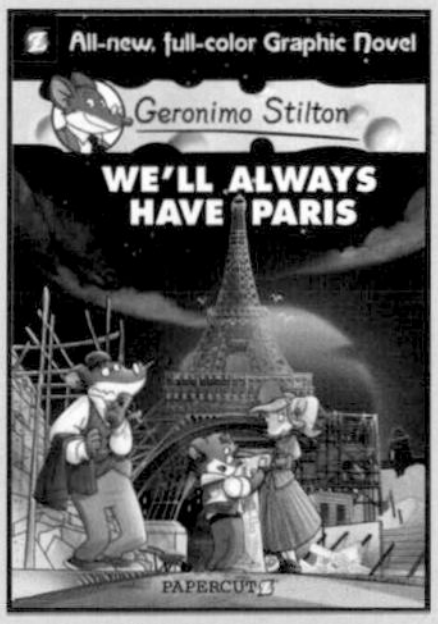
All-new, full-color Graphic Novel
Geronimo Stilton
WE'LL ALWAYS HAVE PARIS
PAPERCUTZ

Graphic Novel #11
"We'll Always Have Paris"

Geronimo Stilton graphic novels are available in hardcover for $9.99 each at booksellers everywhere.

Or order from us: please add $4.00 for postage and handling for the first book, add $1.00 for each additional book.
Please make check payable to NBM Publishing.
Send to: Papercutz 160 Broadway, Suite 700, East Wing,
New York, NY 10038

www.papercutz.com

PROFESSOR VON VOLT IS A FAMOUS SCIENTIST. HE DESIGNED THIS TIME MACHINE FOR THE STILTON FAMILY: THEIR MISSION IS TO DEFEAT THE PIRATE CATS AND SAVE HISTORY!

SPEEDRAT

Geronimo Stilton

FOLLOWING THE TRAIL OF MARCO POLO

By Geronimo Stilton

New York

FOLLOWING THE TRAIL OF MARCO POLO
© EDIZIONI PIEMME 2007 S.p.A.
Via Tiziano 32, 20145
Milan, Italy

Text by Geronimo Stilton
Editorial coordination by Patrizia Puricelli
Original editing by Daniela Finistauri
Script by Demetrio Bargellini
Based on an original idea by Elisabetta Dami
Artistic coordination by Roberta Bianchi
Artistic assistance by Tommaso Valsecchi
Graphic Project by Michela Battaglin
Graphics by Marta Lorini
Cover art and color by Flavio Ferron
Interior illustrations by Giuseppe Facciotto and color by Davide Turotti

Original title: Geronimo Stilton Sulle Tracce di Marco Polo

Translation by: Nanette McGuinness

www.geronimostilton.com

Lettering and Production by Ortho
Michael Petranek – Associate Editor
Jim Salicrup
Editor-in-Chief

ISBN: 978-1-59707-188-8

Printed in China
August 2012 by WKT Co. LTD
3/F Phase I Leader Industrial Centre
188 Texaco Rd., Tsuen Wan, N.T., Hong Kong

Distributed by Macmillan

Fifth Papercutz Printing

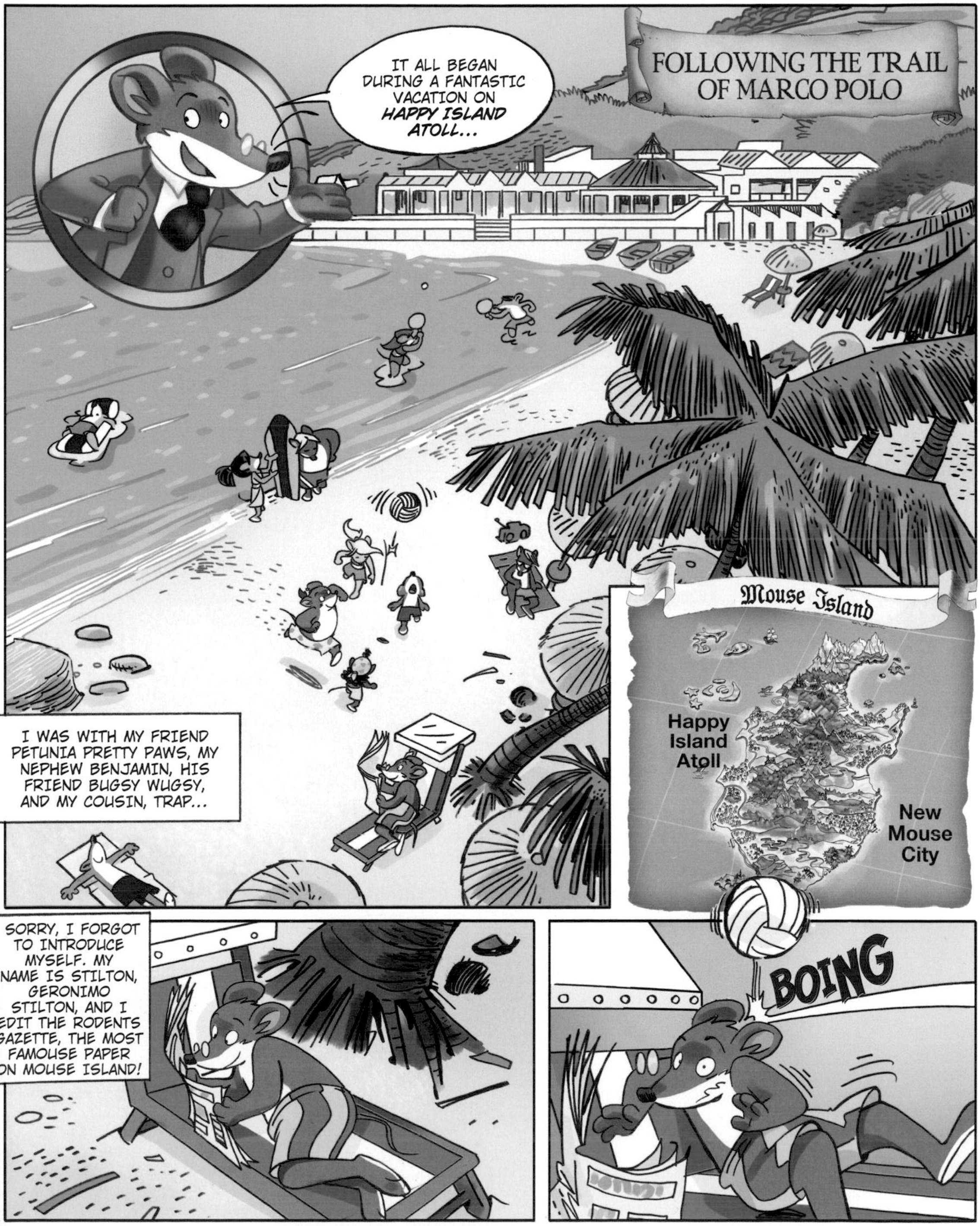
FOLLOWING THE TRAIL OF MARCO POLO
IT ALL BEGAN DURING A FANTASTIC VACATION ON HAPPY ISLAND ATOLL...
Mouse Island
Happy Island Atoll
New Mouse City
I WAS WITH MY FRIEND PETUNIA PRETTY PAWS, MY NEPHEW BENJAMIN, HIS FRIEND BUGSY WUGSY, AND MY COUSIN, TRAP...
SORRY, I FORGOT TO INTRODUCE MYSELF. MY NAME IS STILTON, GERONIMO STILTON, AND I EDIT THE RODENTS GAZETTE, THE MOST FAMOUSE PAPER ON MOUSE ISLAND!
BOING

I WAS ON VACATION, BUT I WASN'T RESTING VERY MUCH. AFTER I GOT HIT BY A BALL, A CRAB PINCHED ME...

...THEN, I WAS BLASTED BY A SANDSTORM...

...AND LAST OF ALL, I WAS MISTAKEN FOR A **FISH** BY A FLOCK OF SEAGULLS!

TO HELP ME RELAX, TRAP PERSUADED ME TO GO WATERSKIING...

STAND UP AS SOON THE SPEEDBOAT TAKES OFF!

UHM... I'LL TRY!

MAYBE IT WOULD'VE BEEN EASIER IF YOU'D PUT SKIS ON ME INSTEAD OF THESE THINGS!

TRUST ME, DEAR COUSIN. THOSE THINGS ARE THE AQUATIC VERSION OF **SNOWBOARDS.**

MAYBE SO... BUT THEY SEEM LIKE TOTALLY NORMAL BEACH TENNIS PADDLES!

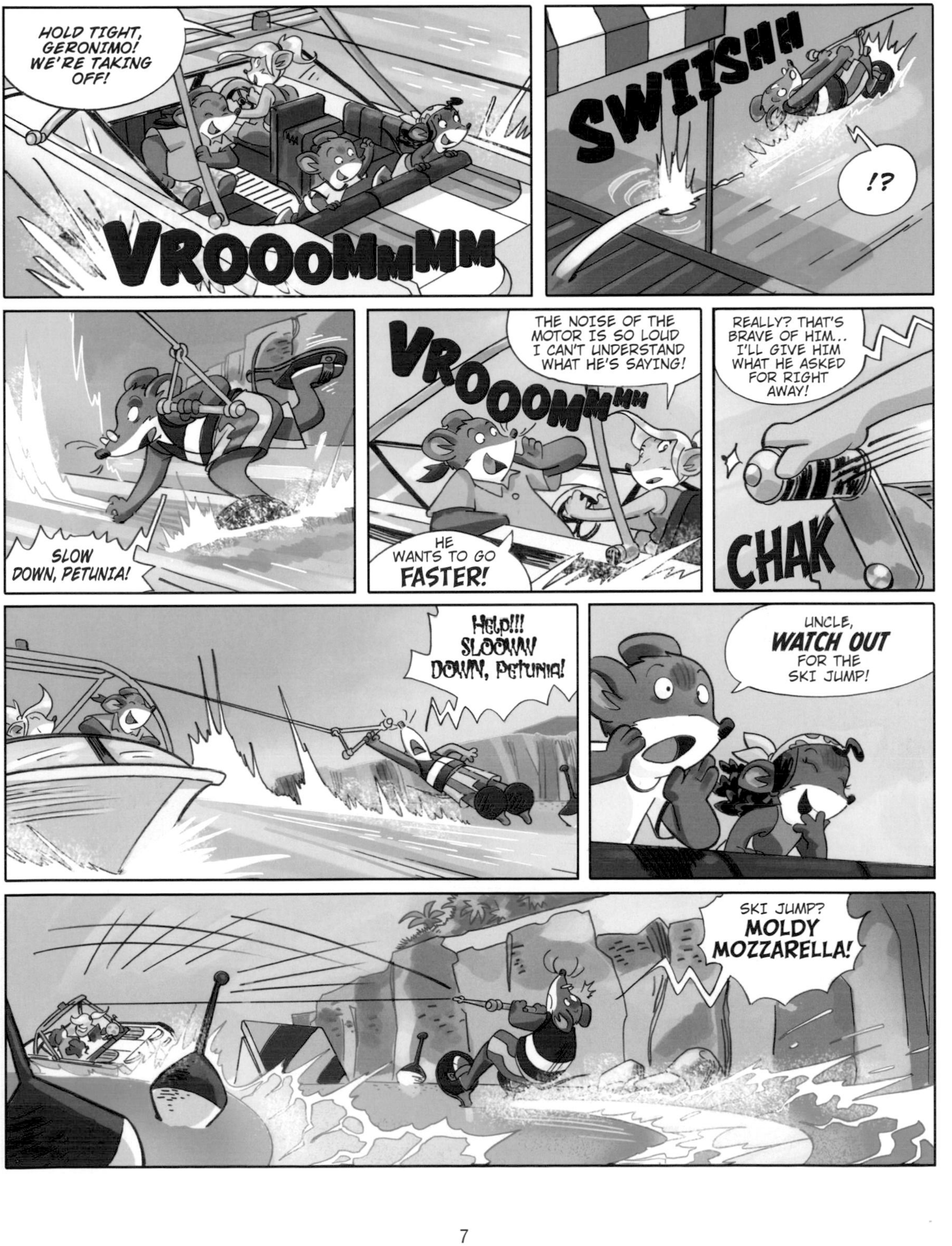
HOLD TIGHT, GERONIMO! WE'RE TAKING OFF!
VROOOMMMMM
SWIISHH
!?
SLOW DOWN, PETUNIA!
VROOOMMMM
THE NOISE OF THE MOTOR IS SO LOUD I CAN'T UNDERSTAND WHAT HE'S SAYING!
HE WANTS TO GO FASTER!
REALLY? THAT'S BRAVE OF HIM... I'LL GIVE HIM WHAT HE ASKED FOR RIGHT AWAY!
CHAK
Help!!! SLOOWW DOWN, Petunia!
UNCLE, WATCH OUT FOR THE SKI JUMP!
SKI JUMP? MOLDY MOZZARELLA!

AAAH!

Rollicking rats!
AMAZING! I'M STILL ALL IN ONE PIECE!

HEY, DID YOU SEE UNCLE GERONIMO'S FANTASTIC JUMP?

I'D BETTER SLOW DOWN! I WOULDN'T WANT HIM TO HURT HIMSELF!

NO, PETUNIA, YOU WORRY TOO MUCH! GERONIMO'S HAVING SO MUCH FUN...

"...WHAT COULD POSSIBLY HAPPEN TO HIM IN THE MIDDLE OF THEOCEAN?"

HUH?

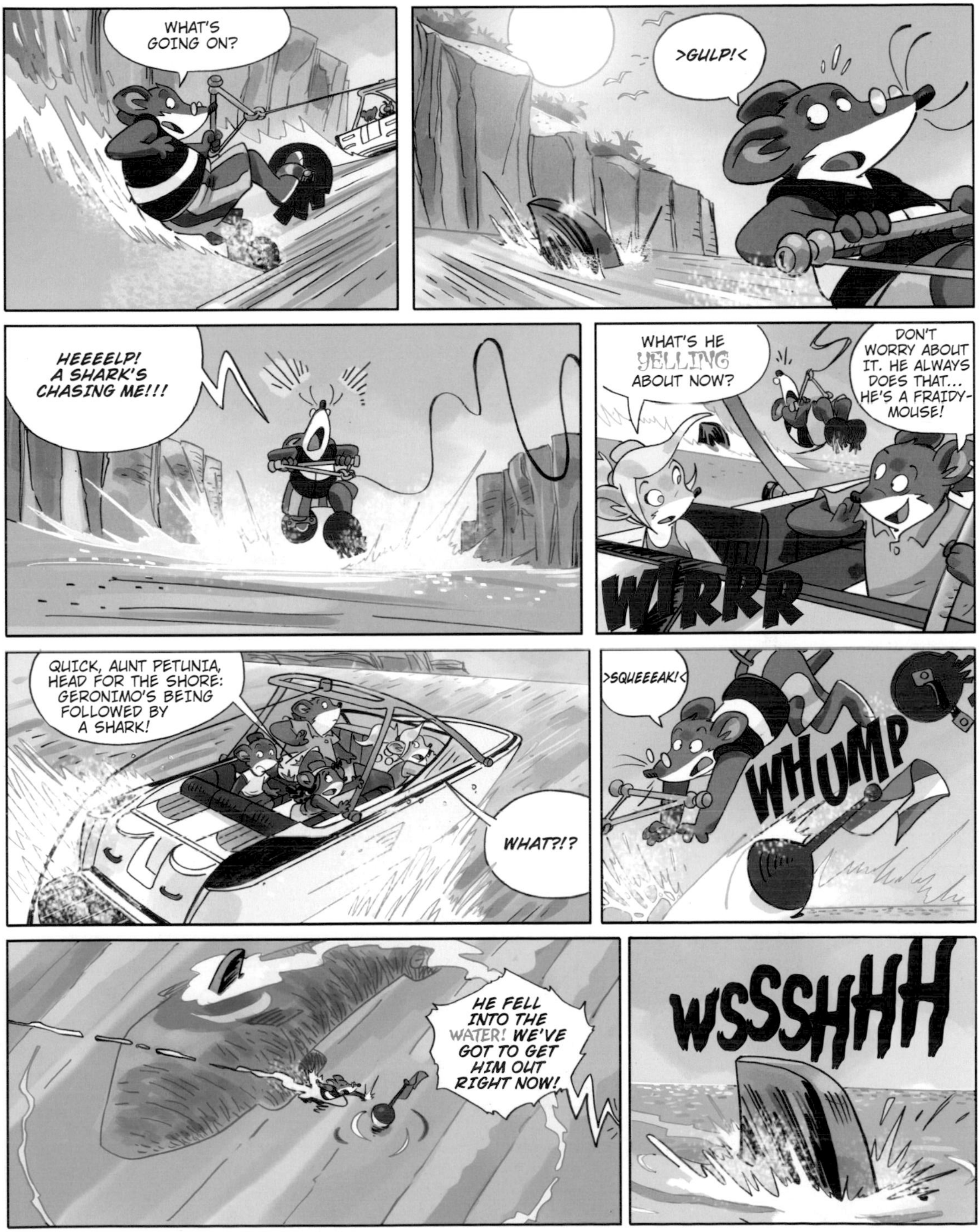

WHAT'S GOING ON?
>GULP!<
HEEEELP! A SHARK'S CHASING ME!!!
WHAT'S HE YELLING ABOUT NOW?
DON'T WORRY ABOUT IT. HE ALWAYS DOES THAT... HE'S A FRAIDY-MOUSE!
WIRRR
QUICK, AUNT PETUNIA, HEAD FOR THE SHORE: GERONIMO'S BEING FOLLOWED BY A SHARK!
WHAT?!?
>SQUEEEAK!<
WHUMP
HE FELL INTO THE WATER! WE'VE GOT TO GET HIM OUT RIGHT NOW!
WSSSHHH

POOR ME! THAT MONSTER'LL *EAT ME* IN A SINGLE MOUTHFUL!

BZZZ... BZZZ... HELLO, GERONIMO!

???

I'M SO SORRY... I DIDN'T MEAN TO *SCARE YOU!!*

WAIT A MINUTE, I KNOW THAT VOICE...PROFESSOR VON VOLT, IS THAT YOU?

BUT...BUT...WHAT ARE YOU DOING IN THE BODY OF A SHARK IN THE MIDDLE OF THE OCEAN?

THIS ISN'T REALLY A SHARK. IT'S ACTUALLY A RADIO-CONTROLLED SUBMARINE THAT I *INVENTED!*

WHILE I'M TALKING TO YOU, I'M SITTING IN MY SECRET LABORATORY IN NEW MOUSE CITY! I NEED YOU AND YOUR FRIENDS TO JOIN ME HERE. IT'S URGENT!

GERONIMO, IS EVERYTHING OKAY? AND WHAT'S THIS?

YES...YES, PETUNIA, THANKS! I'LL EXPLAIN EVERYTHING TO YOU IN JUST A MOMENT!

WE'LL CATCH THE NEXT FLIGHT, PROFESSOR! BUT IT'LL *TAKE* US A LOT OF TIME TO REACH YOU!

CLANG!

I'LL TAKE YOU TO NEW MOUSE CITY ON MY SUBMARINE: IT'S SUPER FAST!

A LITTLE LATER, EVERYONE WAS ON BOARD...

PROFESSOR VON VOLT NEVER CEASES TO AMAZE ME!

ONLY A **GENIUS** LIKE HIM COULD BUILD A SUBMARINE IN THE SHAPE OF A SHARK!

AND THERE'S EVEN A FRIDGE FULL OF **CHEESE!**

IT MUST BE SOMETHING REALLY SERIOUS IF HE CAME LOOKING FOR US WHILE WE WERE ON VACATION!

YES, YOU'RE RIGHT!

WHATEVER THE REASON HE CALLED US, WE'LL FIND OUT SOON! HERE WE ARE AT NEW MOUSE CITY HARBOR!

HEY, LOOK OUT! THE SUBMARINE IS GOING TO CRASH INTO THAT ROCK!

WHiRRR

B-BUT... THERE'S A DOOR OPENING UP IN THE **ROCK** UNDER THE LIGHTHOUSE!

11

WELCOME! I HOPE YOU HAD A NICE TRIP!

HEY! THIS TIME THE LAB IS RIGHT UNDER THE NEW MOUSE CITY LIGHTHOUSE!

IT WAS A RAT-TASTIC TRIP!

WERE YOU THINKING OF BRINGING THAT FRIDGE WITH YOU, TRAP?

OF COURSE! YOU WOULDN'T WANT TO LEAVE THIS DELICIOUS CHEESE HERE!

I'M SORRY I BOTHERED YOU, BUT I DIDN'T HAVE ANY CHOICE: THE PIRATE CATS ARE BACK IN ACTION!

THE P-PIRATE CATS?

THEM AGAIN!

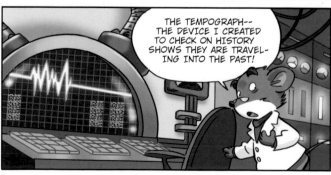

THE TEMPOGRAPH-- THE DEVICE I CREATED TO CHECK ON HISTORY SHOWS THEY ARE TRAVELING INTO THE PAST!

THOSE CHEESE HEADS ARE TRYING TO CHANGE HISTORY TO THEIR ADVANTAGE AGAIN!

TELL US, WHERE ARE THEY HEADED THIS TIME, PROFESSOR?

THEY'RE HEADING FOR *KHANBALIK*, THE CAPITAL OF ANCIENT CHINA! AND THEY CHOSE THE YEAR *1292!*

CHINA

IS A NATION IN EAST ASIA. ITS TERRITORY HAS BEEN INHABITED BY HUMANS SINCE ANTIQUITY AND HAS MANY PREHISTORIC ARCHAEOLOGICAL SITES. IT WASN'T UNTIL THE 3RD CENTURY B.C. THAT THE QIN DYNASTY UNIFIED THE DIFFERENT POPULATIONS THAT LIVED IN THE REGION AND CREATED THE FIRST CHINESE EMPIRE. CONSTRUCTION OF THE GREAT WALL BEGAN DURING THIS PERIOD. TODAY, CHINA IS ONE OF THE BIGGEST COUNTRIES IN THE WORLD: ITS SURFACE AREA IS OVER NINE MILLION SQUARE KILOMETERS AND IT HAS OVER A BILLION INHABITANTS. ITS CAPITAL IS BEIJING, WHICH WAS CALLED KHANBALIK AT THE TIME OF OUR STORY.

>SLURP!< CHEESE! AND WHAT ARE THESE? **CHOCOLATES?**

HMM...WHY DID THEY CHOOSE THAT PLACE AND THAT TIME?

I DON'T KNOW...

...BUT AT THAT TIME, THE FAMOUS MERCHANT AND TRAVELER *MARCO POLO* COULD BE FOUND IN CHINA!

MARCO POLO (1254-1324)

WAS BORN IN VENICE, ITALY, TO A FAMILY OF MERCHANTS. IN 1271, MARCO POLO LEFT FOR CHINA WITH HIS FATHER, NICCOLO, AND HIS UNCLE MATTEO. THERE THEY STAYED AT THE COURT OF THE MONGOLIAN EMPEROR, KUBLAI KHAN, WHO ENTRUSTED THEM WITH MANY COMMISSIONS AND DIPLOMATIC MISSIONS. AFTER 17 YEARS IN CHINA, MARCO RETURNED TO VENICE IN 1292 WITH HIS FAMILY AND RELATIVES. THE TALES OF HIS JOURNEY AND HIS STAY IN CHINA ARE COLLECTED IN THE BOOK, THE TRAVELS OF MARCO POLO.

COULD MARCO POLO REALLY BE THE PIRATE CATS' TARGET?

TO FIND THAT OUT, WE'LL JUST HAVE TO **LEAVE** TOO!

A LITTLE LATER, WE WERE ON THE SPEEDRAT...

YOU'LL FIND **CLOTHES** ON BOARD SO YOU CAN DRESS LIKE A VENETIAN MERCHANT OF THAT PERIOD!

AH, I ALMOST FORGOT TO GIVE YOU MY SPECIAL EAR-PHONES THAT LET YOU UNDER-STAND AND SPEAK THE LOCAL LANGUAGE!

I CAN'T FIND THEM...WHERE DID I PUT THEM? I WAS SURE I LEFT THEM NEXT TO THE... CHEESE??

BY THE FLEA-RIDDEN FUR OF A WERECAT! THE CHEESE AND THE EARPHONES HAVE DISAPPEARED!

>BURP!<

?!?

I C-C-CAN'T BELIEVE IT! YOUR COUSIN ATE THEM!

TRAP! COULD YOU HAVE SWALLOWED SOMETHING LIKE THAT?

UMM...THEY LOOKED LIKE CHOCOLATES!

WHAT ARE WE GOING TO DO NOW? WITHOUT THE EAR- PHONES, WE WON'T UNDERSTAND A WORD!

HMM... LET'S SEE...LET ME THINK FOR A MOMENT...

BUT OF COURSE! I'M SUCH A NITWIT...I'LL GIVE YOU THE SPARES!

SOMETIMES THE PROFESSOR IS REALLY ABSENT- MINDED...HEE, HEE, HEE!

RIGHT! HE ALWAYS FORGETS EVERYTHING!

SO WE WERE FINALLY READY TO GO...

ZZZZOOOOOM

BREAK A PAW,✱ FRIENDS! THE PRESENT AND THE FUTURE ARE IN YOUR HANDS!

✱ GOOD LUCK

14

MEANWHILE, CATARDONE III, RULER OF THE PIRATE CATS, HIS DAUGHTER, TERSILLA, AND THEIR ASSISTANT, BONZO, HAD ARRIVED IN CHINA, IN THE YEAR 1292...

TERSILLA, DO YOU THINK IT WOULD BE GOOD TO HIDE THE CATJET IN THE VICINITY OF THE GREAT WALL?

THE GREAT WALL WAS BEGUN IN THE THIRD CENTURY B.C. BY EMPEROR QIN SHI HUANG TO PROTECT CHINA FROM INVASIONS BY THE VARIOUS NOMADIC TRIBES WHO CAME FROM OUTSIDE THE COUNTRY. IT'S MORE THAN 6,000 KILOMETERS TALL-- BETWEEN 5 AND 10 METERS LONG--AND WIDE ENOUGH FOR CARTS TO DRIVE ON LIKE A ROAD.

YES, THAT'S AN EXCELLENT HIDING PLACE! PLUS, WE'RE JUST A FEW KILOMETERS FROM KHANBALIK, THE CAPITAL OF THE EMPIRE!

CATJET

I THOUGHT THE GREAT WALL WAS ALWAYS FULL OF TOURISTS!

IT WILL BE IN THE FUTURE, DADDY DEAR, BUT AS YOU SEE, IT'S DESERTED AT THE MOMENT.

BUT OF COURSE, I GET IT...WE RETURNED TO THE PAST TO BOOST TOURISM AT THE GREAT WALL!

GOOD IDEA! TO START WITH, LET'S BUILD A FIVE-STAR HOTEL!

SURE! THE HOTEL "CATARDONE!"

AND A SUPER-DELUXE RESTAURANT NEARBY!

AND A FAIR-GROUND!

QUIIIIIET, YOU TWO!!!

WE'RE DOING NOTHING OF THE KIND! THE MISSION OBJECTIVE IS SOMETHING ELSE!

AH, REALLY?

TOO BAD!

HOW MANY TIMES DO I HAVE TO TELL YOU: WE HAVE TO STEAL THE *diary* OF MARCO POLO, THE GREAT VENETIAN VOYAGER!

WHAT ARE WE GOING TO DO WITH A DIARY?

IT'S JUST A *pile* OF PAPER!

WE'LL PUBLISH IT OURSELVES, SO WE CAN TAKE CREDIT FOR HIS TRAVELS! THAT WAY, THE PIRATE CATS' NAME WILL BE FAMOUS THROUGHOUT THE CENTURIES!

HMM...OF COURSE...

ON THE HOTEL ROOF THERE SHOULD BE A HELICOPTER PAD!

SURE! AND ALSO ONE FOR HOT AIR BALLOONS!

GRRR!

I TOLD YOU TO BE QUIET!!!

16

WE'LL DO WHAT I SAID! STOP MOUSING OFF!*

*TALKING NONSENSE

PHEW...OKAY! BUT HOW ARE WE GOING TO GET NEAR THIS MARCO POLO?

I THOUGHT YOU'D STUDIED UP BEFORE LEAVING, DADDY DEAR!

STU...? WHAT DO YOU MEAN, TERSILLA?

STUDIED, MY EMPEROR, MEANS...

I KNOW PERFECTLY WELL WHAT IT MEANS, *YOU HAIRBALL!* I DON'T NEED A LESSON!

SMACK

AT THIS TIME, CHINA WAS PART OF THE MONGOLIAN EMPIRE! EMPEROR KUBLAI KHAN HOSTED MARCO POLO, HIS FATHER, AND HIS UNCLE!

MONGOLIANS

MONGOLIANS WERE A NOMADIC WARRIOR PEOPLE WHO LIVED IN VARIOUS REGIONS OF CENTRAL ASIA. IN THE EARLY 1200S, THE FAMOUS LEADER GENGHIS KHAN (AROUND 1167-1227) SUCCEEDED IN UNIFYING THE DIFFERENT TRIBES AND BEGAN A WAR OF CONQUEST THAT LED THEM TO OCCUPY THE MAJORITY OF THE CONTINENT OF ASIA, CREATING THE GREATEST EMPIRE HISTORY HAS EVER RECORDED. AFTER GENGHIS KHAN'S DEATH, THE EMPIRE CONTINUED TO EXIST, LASTING UNTIL 1336. TODAY THE DESCENDANTS OF THE MONGOLIAN PEOPLE LIVE IN MONGOLIA, A NATION ON THE BORDER OF CHINA.

TO GET NEAR HIM, WE'LL PRESENT OURSELVES TO COURT, PRETENDING TO BE VENETIAN MERCHANTS! THEN IT'LL BE CHILD'S PLAY TO STEAL THE DIARY!

IS EVERYTHING CLEAR NOW OR DO I HAVE TO EXPLAIN IT TO YOU AGAIN?

YES, YES... THAT IS... NO, THAT IS...

STOP CHATTERING! LET'S PUT ON OUR MOUSE MASKS AND CHANGE CLOTHES!

THIS TIME, NO ONE WILL BE ABLE TO *DERAIL US!*

A LITTLE LATER, ON THE WAY TO KHANBALIK...

COME ON! WALK!

I'M TIRED! IS IT MUCH FARTHER?

IF WE HAD HORSES, IT WOULD BE A LOT EASIER!

LOOK! WE COULD TAKE THOSE DONKEYS OVER THERE!

THOSE AREN'T DONKEYS! THEY'RE PRZEWALSKI'S HORSES!

PRZEWALSKI'S HORSES

ARE A TYPE OF HORSE NATIVE TO MONGOLIA. THEY HAVE A MASSIVE HEAD, WITH SMALL EYES AND EARS, A SQUAT BODY AND A SHORT BRISTLY MANE. THEIR LEGS AND MUZZLES ARE DARKER THAN THE REST OF THEIR BODIES. THE PHYSICAL FEATURES OF THIS HORSE HAVE STAYED THE SAME FROM PREHISTORY TO OUR TIME.

THERE ARE EXACTLY THREE...LIKE US! WHAT DO YOU SAY?

AND HOW ARE WE GOING TO...?

I'LL *RUSH* OVER RIGHT NOW TO CAPTURE THEM! IT'LL JUST TAKE ME A MINUTE!

BONZO, WAIT!

CHARRRGE!!!

NO, STOP! DON'T RUN AWAY! COME HERE!

CLOP CLOP

>PHEW<...WHAT HARD WORK! BUT WHERE ARE THOSE HORSES HIDING?

WHAT'S THAT NOISE?

RUSTLE

AAAAH! A PANDA!

ZOOOM

W-WHY IS THAT GIANT PANDA RUNNING TOWARDS US?

>GULP!<

THE GIANT PANDA
BELONGS TO THE BEAR FAMILY AND EATS ALMOST EXCLUSIVE-LY BAMBOO. NATIVE TO CENTRAL CHINA, IT CAN ALSO BE FOUND IN THE MOUNTAINOUS REGIONS OF SZECHUAN AND TIBET. TODAY THE PANDA IS AN ENDANGERED SPECIES.

LET'S SCRAM!

HEY, YOU TWO, WAIT FOR ME!

HELPPPP!

A LITTLE LATER...

>HMFF, HMFF<... IF I RUN ANOTHER FOOT, I'LL **BURST!!**

OF COURSE...BUT LUCKILY THE PANDA STOPPED FOLLOWING US AT THE GATES OF KHANBALIK!

>PANT... PANT...<

HUH? YOU SAID KHANBALIK? SO YOU'RE SAYING THAT WE'VE ARRIVED, TERSILLA?

RIGHT, DADDY DEAR!

**KHANBALIK
(THE CITY OF KHAN)**

WAS THE MONGOLIAN NAME USED FOR THE CITY THAT TODAY WE CALL BEIJING. THE FIRST CITY CENTER DATES BACK TO THE 5TH CENTURY B.C. AND WAS FORMED FROM A GROUP OF SMALL VILLAGES. OVER TIME, THE CITY GREW IN IMPORTANCE UNTIL THE MONGOLS CHOSE IT AS THE CAPITAL OF THEIR EMPIRE IN 1267.

HAVE YOU NOTICED EVERYONE'S **LOOKING** AT US?

REMEMBER WE LOOK LIKE VENETIAN MERCHANTS! NOW LET'S GO PRESENT OURSELVES AT COURT!

AT THE COURT OF THE GREAT KHAN...

LET THE FOREIGNERS ENTER!

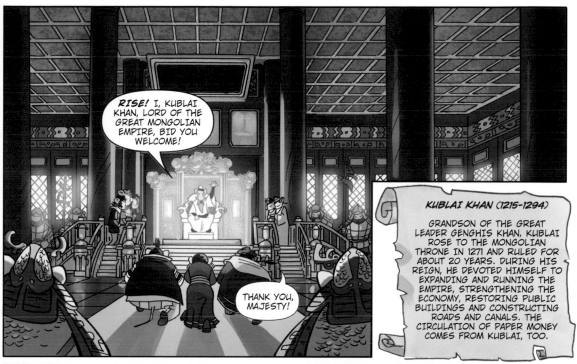

RISE! I, KUBLAI KHAN, LORD OF THE GREAT MONGOLIAN EMPIRE, BID YOU WELCOME!

THANK YOU, MAJESTY!

KUBLAI KHAN (1215-1294)

GRANDSON OF THE GREAT LEADER GENGHIS KHAN, KUBLAI ROSE TO THE MONGOLIAN THRONE IN 1271 AND RULED FOR ABOUT 20 YEARS. DURING HIS REIGN, HE DEVOTED HIMSELF TO EXPANDING AND RUNNING THE EMPIRE, STRENGTHENING THE ECONOMY, RESTORING PUBLIC BUILDINGS AND CONSTRUCTING ROADS AND CANALS. THE CIRCULATION OF PAPER MONEY COMES FROM KUBLAI, TOO.

I AM ALWAYS HAPPY TO WELCOME FOREIGN TRAVELERS! THEY CAN LEARN MANY THINGS FROM ENCOUNTERING OTHER CULTURES!

AND YOU AND YOUR LOVED ONES KNOW THIS WELL, CORRECT, MARCO?

YES, MY LORD!

MARCO? THEN HE MUST BE *MARCO POLO!*

YOU'RE MARCO POLO, WHO LEFT VENICE 20 YEARS AGO WITH YOUR FATHER, NICCOLO, AND YOUR UNCLE, MATTEO?

THAT'S RIGHT! BUT...HOW DID YOU GET TO KNOW MY NAME?

OH, IN **VENICE**, THE CITY WE COME FROM, THE POLO NAME IS VERY FAMOUS!

B-BUT THEN ARE YOU MY COUNTRY-MEN? IT'S SUCH A PLEASURE TO MEET YOU! WHAT'S YOUR NAME?

MY NAME IS RATILLA RATINI AND THIS IS MY FATHER RATARDONE AND OUR FRIEND RATONZO RATON. WE'RE MERCHANTS!

VERY PLEASED TO MEET YOU! THIS IS MY FATHER, NICCOLO, AND MY UNCLE, MATTEO!

WELCOME!

TELL US, WHAT'S THE NEWS FROM VENICE?

DOES OUR BELOVED CITY STILL HAVE THE MOST POWERFUL FLEET ON ALL THE SEAS?

VENICE
DURING MARCO POLO'S TIME, ITALY WAS DIVIDED INTO MANY SMALL STATES, AND THE CITY OF VENICE WAS A SEPARATE, RICH AND POWERFUL REPUBLIC. DUE TO ITS ADVANTAGEOUS POSITION ON THE SEA, IT HAD A LARGE NAVAL FLEET DEVOTED TO COMMERCE ALONG THE ADRIATIC AND MEDITERRANEAN SEAS.

VENICE

WELL, NOW... IT SEEMS TO ME THAT...AH, YES...THE FLEET **SANK!**

THAT'S RIGHT, BUT...THEY REPLACED IT WITH HELICOPTERS!

WHAT? THE ENTIRE FLEET SANK?

HELICOPTERS? WHAT COULD THESE HELICOPTERS BE?

PLEASE FORGIVE THEM! THEY'RE WORN OUT FROM THE JOURNEY AND DON'T KNOW WHAT THEY'RE SAYING!

>MMPH!<

IN FACT, IF THE GREAT KHAN WILL PERMIT IT, WE'D LIKE TO GO AND REST!

AS YOU WISH! I SHALL ORDER A ROOM BE PREPARED FOR YOU IN THE APARTMENTS RESERVED FOR GUESTS! **UNTIL LATER!**

AT EXACTLY THE SAME MOMENT, NOT FAR FROM KHANBALIK...

VRROOOOMM

BRAKE, TRAP! WE'RE GOING TO HIT SOMETHING!

I'M TRYING!

WHRRRRR

THE RICE PADDIES! THE RICE PADDIES!

BABOOOMMM

SKREEECH

DID YOU SEE THAT PERFECT LANDING? YOU DIDN'T NEED TO GET ALL WORKED UP!

>SIGH<

NEXT TIME, LET PETUNIA DRIVE, PLEASE!

WHAT ARE YOU COMPLAINING ABOUT, COUSIN? LOOK, THE FRIDGE IS SAFE AND SOUND!

ROLLICKING RATS! WHY DID YOU BRING IT? THERE AREN'T ANY ELECTRICAL APPLIANCES IN THIS PERIOD!

I KNOW, BUT WHO KNOWS? MAYBE IT'LL TURN OUT TO BE USEFUL TO US, AND NO ONE WILL NOTICE IT INSIDE THIS BAG!

IT WOULD BE GOOD TO GET GOING NOW! THE PIRATE CATS ALREADY HAVE ENOUGH OF AN ADVANTAGE!

YOU'RE RIGHT, PATTY, WE'D BETTER NOT LOSE ANY MORE TIME! LET'S GO!

AFTER A QUICK CHANGE OF CLOTHES...

>SIGH<...THIS TIME PROFESSOR VON VOLT DIDN'T GUESS THE RIGHT SIZE!

TEE, HEE, HEE!

I'LL ROLL UP YOUR SLEEVES LIKE THIS SO YOU'LL BE MORE COMFORTABLE!

UM...THANKS, PETUNIA!

UNCLE GERONIMO, WHERE CAN WE HIDE THE TIME MACHINE?

WHAT DO YOU THINK OF PUTTING IT IN THIS BAMBOO GROVE? IT SHOULDN'T ATTRACT ATTENTION THERE!

THAT SEEMS PERFECT TO ME!

AFTER HIDING THE SPEEDRAT, WE FINALLY SET OUT...

THESE RICE PADDIES ARE SO PEACEFUL...

HELPPPPP! WHO CAN HELP ME???

???

MAYBE YOU SPOKE TOO SOON!

GET OFF YOUR HORSE, RIGHT NOW!

HEY LOOK! THAT RODENT IS IN **DANGER!**

GIVE US ALL YOUR MONEY, RODENT!

HOW DARE YOU, SCOUNDRELS? I'M AN IMPERIAL OFFICIAL: THE GREAT KHAN WILL PUNISH YOU FOR THIS!

GET YOUR PAWS OFF HIM!

?

FOR ALL THE EMPEROR'S RICE! FOREIGNERS!

TAKE THAT!

WOOSH

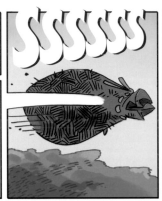

SSSSSSS

BONK!

SQUEEEAK!

OOPS! I AIMED WRONG...

LET'S GET OUT OF HERE! THESE FOREIGNERS ARE A BIT STRANGE!

I'M SO SORRY, COUSIN... I WANTED TO HIT THE THIEVES NOT YOU!

>GROAN!<

WAS THAT WHAT YOU HAD IN MIND WHEN YOU SAID THE FRIDGE MIGHT BE USEFUL TO US?

NO, I ASSURE YOU!

ARE YOU HURT?

NO, AND IT'S ALL THANKS TO YOU! WHO ARE YOU? WHERE ARE YOU FROM?

ALLOW ME TO MAKE THE INTRODUCTIONS! MY NAME IS STILTONIN, GERONIMO STILTONIN...

...AND THESE ARE MY FRIENDS: MISTRESS * PETUNIANA, BUGSORAMA, BENJAMINO, AND TRAPOLON! WE'RE MERCHANTS AND WE COME FROM VENICE!

*MISTRESS/ MISS, IN OLD ITALIAN.

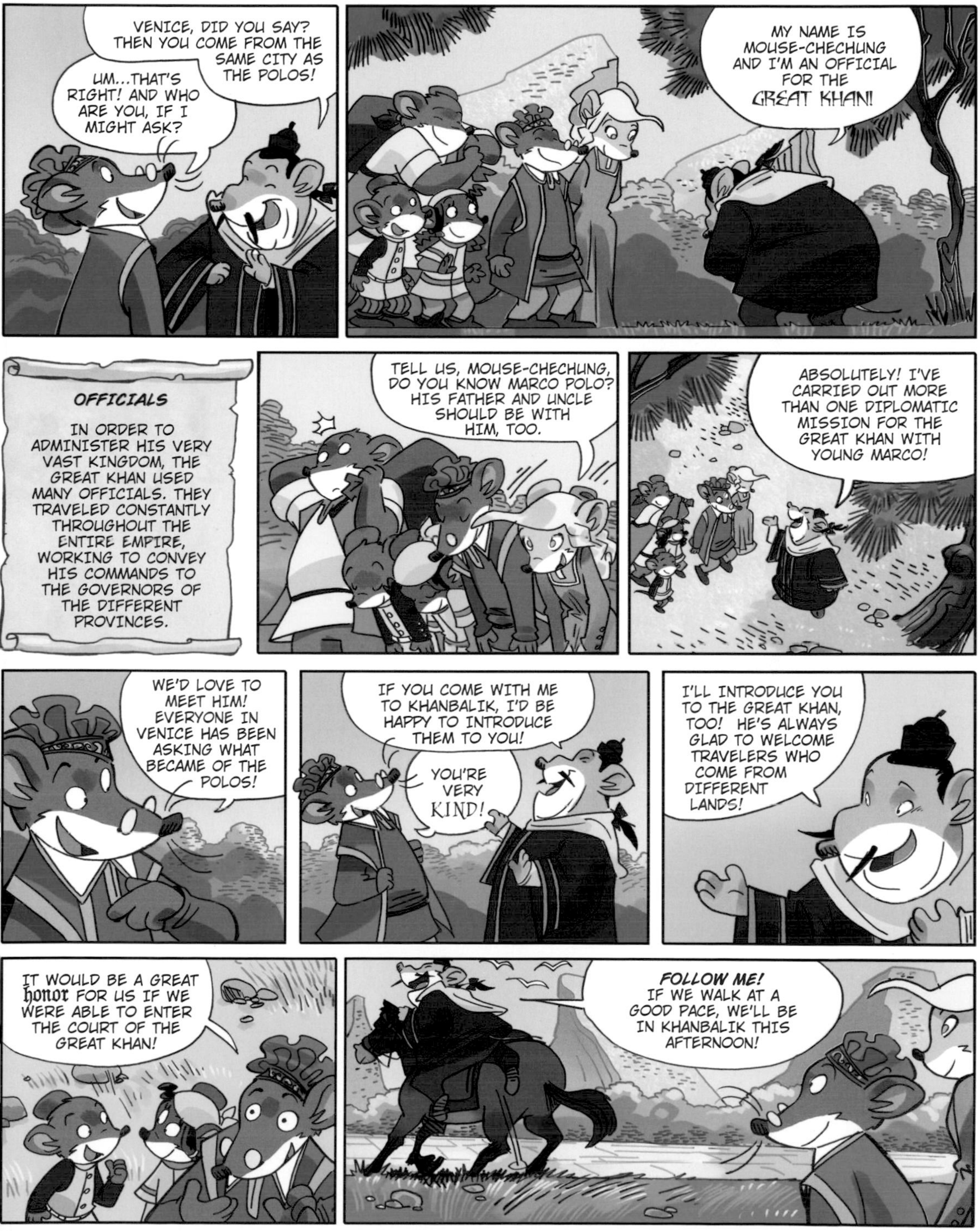
VENICE, DID YOU SAY? THEN YOU COME FROM THE SAME CITY AS THE POLOS!
UM...THAT'S RIGHT! AND WHO ARE YOU, IF I MIGHT ASK?
MY NAME IS MOUSE-CHECHUNG AND I'M AN OFFICIAL FOR THE GREAT KHAN!
OFFICIALS
IN ORDER TO ADMINISTER HIS VERY VAST KINGDOM, THE GREAT KHAN USED MANY OFFICIALS. THEY TRAVELED CONSTANTLY THROUGHOUT THE ENTIRE EMPIRE, WORKING TO CONVEY HIS COMMANDS TO THE GOVERNORS OF THE DIFFERENT PROVINCES.
TELL US, MOUSE-CHECHUNG, DO YOU KNOW MARCO POLO? HIS FATHER AND UNCLE SHOULD BE WITH HIM, TOO.
ABSOLUTELY! I'VE CARRIED OUT MORE THAN ONE DIPLOMATIC MISSION FOR THE GREAT KHAN WITH YOUNG MARCO!
WE'D LOVE TO MEET HIM! EVERYONE IN VENICE HAS BEEN ASKING WHAT BECAME OF THE POLOS!
IF YOU COME WITH ME TO KHANBALIK, I'D BE HAPPY TO INTRODUCE THEM TO YOU!
YOU'RE VERY KIND!
I'LL INTRODUCE YOU TO THE GREAT KHAN, TOO! HE'S ALWAYS GLAD TO WELCOME TRAVELERS WHO COME FROM DIFFERENT LANDS!
IT WOULD BE A GREAT HONOR FOR US IF WE WERE ABLE TO ENTER THE COURT OF THE GREAT KHAN!
FOLLOW ME! IF WE WALK AT A GOOD PACE, WE'LL BE IN KHANBALIK THIS AFTERNOON!

SO WE ARRIVED AT THE IMPERIAL PALACE IN THE MAGNIFICENT ROYAL CITY OF KHANBALIK...

THE IMPERIAL PALACE

ROSE FROM INSIDE A DOUBLY WALLED-IN AREA. BASED ON MARCO POLO'S DESCRIPTION, IT WAS IMMENSE, AND THE WALLS OF ITS ROOMS WERE COVERED WITH SILVER AND GOLD. THERE WERE GARDENS AND A LAKE, FED BY A RIVER. IN ADDITION, JUST BEHIND THE PALACE, THE KHAN HAD BUILT AN ARTIFICIAL HILL, ON WHICH TREES FROM EVERY REGION IN THE EMPIRE WERE PLANTED.

...HOME OF KUBLAI KHAN, LORD OF THE VASTEST EMPIRE HISTORY HAS EVER RECORDED!

MORE VENETIAN MERCHANTS HAVE ARRIVED?

THIS IS REALLY A DAY OF SURPRISES!

?!?

IT'S A PITY... ANOTHER THREE VENETIAN MERCHANTS ARRIVED AT COURT TODAY, BUT THEY'VE JUST LEFT FOR THE CITY OF QUINSAI, ALONG WITH MARCO POLO!

QUINSAI

WAS THE ANCIENT NAME OF THE MODERN-DAY CITY OF HANGZHOU. BUILT ON THE YANGTZE RIVER DELTA (THE BLUE RIVER), ITS LANDSCAPE LOOKS A LOT LIKE VENICE, WITH MANY BRIDGES AND CANALS. MARCO POLO WAS VERY FOND OF THE SPOT AND SPOKE OF IT AS ONE OF THE MOST BEAUTIFUL AND NOBLE CITIES IN THE WORLD.

ANYHOW, I'M SURE MY FRIENDS NICCOLO AND MATTEO POLO WILL BE GOOD COMPANY FOR YOU!

DID YOU HEAR? MARCO POLO LEFT!

ALONG WITH--THREE VENETIAN MERCHANTS!

AS A REWARD FOR THE COURAGE YOU SHOWED AGAINST THE BANDITS, I'M INVITING YOU TO MY BANQUET THIS EVENING! YOU'LL BE THE GUESTS OF HONOR!

THANK YOU, MAJESTY! WE'LL BE GLAD TO ATTEND!

HURRAY! WE'RE FINALLY GOING TO EAT! YUM!

A LITTLE LATER, MOUSE-CHECHUNG ACCOMPANIED US TO THE APARTMENTS RESERVED FOR GUESTS...

THIS SERVANT WILL LEAD YOU TO YOUR ROOMS! WE'LL SEE EACH OTHER THIS EVENING AT THE EMPEROR'S BANQUET!

THANK YOU FOR EVERYTHING, MOUSE-CHECHUNG! SEE YOU THIS EVENING!

A LITTLE LATER, WE MET UP IN PETUNIA'S ROOM SO WE COULD TAKE STOCK OF THE SITUATION, FAR FROM PRYING EYES AND EARS...

DO YOU SMELL THE STINK OF THE PIRATE CATS, TOO?

WHO KNOWS WHERE THEY ARE...?

WHEN KUBLAI KHAN MENTIONED THREE MERCHANTS, A **SHIVER** RAN ALONG MY FUR!

PHEW! YOU'RE A REGULAR 'FRAIDY-MOUSE, COUSIN!

BUT THEIR ARRIVAL IS A REALLY STRANGE COINCIDENCE! WE SHOULD **INVESTIGATE!**

I AGREE WITH YOU, *PETUNIA!*

IMAGINE IF YOU DIDN'T!

>PHEW...< WHERE WERE THE THREE MER- CHANTS HEADED?

TO *CHUNCHAI,* I THINK...

NO, IT WAS QUINSAI!

AND MARCO POLO WAS WITH THEM!

THAT'S STRANGE, TOO! THEY'VE JUST BARELY ARRIVED FROM A LONG JOURNEY AND HAVE ALREADY LEFT AGAIN! IT ALMOST SEEMS AS IF...

...THEY DIDN'T WANT TO LOSE SIGHT OF MARCO POLO!

IT REALLY SEEMS LIKE...BUT IF THIS IS REALLY ABOUT THE PIRATE CATS, WHAT CAN THEY WANT WITH HIM?

THE ONLY WAY TO KNOW IS FOR US TO GO TO QUINSAI TOO, AND KEEP OUR EYES WIDE OPEN! THEY COULD BE ANYWHERE!

THAT'S FINE WITH ME, BUT NOT BEFORE THE GREAT KHAN'S BANQUET: THE FRIDGE IS ALMOST **EMPTY!**

TSK!

THAT EVENING, DURING THE MAGNIFICENT BANQUET GIVEN BY THE EMPEROR...

...I TOOK ADVANTAGE OF THE OPPORTUNITY TO CONSULT WITH MOUSE-CHECHUNG AND THE POLO BROTHERS.

SO YOU WANT TO GO TO THE CITY OF QUINSAI, TOO?

WE'D LIKE TO VISIT IT AND MEET YOUR *SON*!

WOW! YOU'RE REALLY TIRELESS TRAVELERS!

THE ROUTE IS RATHER LONG: IT WILL TAKE AROUND A MONTH ON HORSEBACK! WHEN DO YOU WANT TO LEAVE?

TOMORROW **MORNING** IF POSSIBLE!

IT SHOULD BE. I'LL TALK TO THE KHAN ABOUT IT. I THINK HE'LL AGREE I SHOULD GO WITH YOU MYSELF!

THANKS, MOUSE-CHECHUNG, YOU'RE A REAL GENTLE-MOUSE!

31

THE FOLLOWING DAY, HAVING GOTTEN THE KHAN'S PERMISSION, WE STARTED OFF...

HOW COME MARCO POLO LEFT THE COURT OF THE KHAN TO GO TO QUINSAI?

MARCO **ADORES** THAT CITY! HE GOES TO VISIT IT VERY OFTEN!

AND NOW, SINCE HE'LL BE RETURNING TO EUROPE SOON, HE ASKED THE GREAT KHAN TO LET HIM SEE IT ONE LAST TIME!

SO MARCO AND HIS **FAMILY** HAVE ALREADY ARRANGED TO GO BACK TO VENICE?

YES, THE POLOS HAVE WANTED TO FOR SOME TIME NOW! BUT THE KHAN IS VERY ATTACHED TO THEM AND DIDN'T WANT TO PART FROM THEM!

IT WAS ONLY A FEW DAYS AGO THAT HE GAVE HIS AGREEMENT TO LET THEM LEAVE FOR VENICE!

I UNDERSTAND THE POLOS. I, TOO, WOULDN'T WANT TO STAY FAR AWAY FOREVER FROM NEW MOUSE... AHEM... FROM VENICE!

OF COURSE... AS ONE OF OUR PROVERBS SAYS, "THERE'S A TIME TO FISH AND A TIME TO BRING IN THE NETS!" AND NOW IS THE TIME FOR THEM TO RETURN!

THE FOLLOWING DAY, WE RODE FROM DAWN TO DUSK, STOPPING ONLY TO REST AND CHANGE HORSES...

THE NETWORK OF ROADS
THE MONGOLIAN EMPIRE HAD A SYSTEM OF ROADS THAT WAS VERY ADVANCED FOR THE TIME. STREETS RAN FROM KHANBALIK TO THE ENTIRE EMPIRE, PASSABLE ON FOOT OR HORSEBACK. ALONG THE ROADS WERE STATIONS WHERE THE KHAN'S MESSENGERS COULD REST AND CHANGE HORSES BEFORE CONTINUING ON TOWARDS THEIR DESTINATIONS.

THE JOURNEY WAS PEACEFUL, EXCEPT FOR A FEW TINY INCIDENTS...

YIIIKES!

AAHHHHH!

CLOMP

CLOMP

CLOMP

AAHHH! HELP!

MEANWHILE, WITH A DAY'S HEAD START BEFORE WE LEFT, THE PIRATE CATS HAD REACHED QUINSAI...

...AND HAD SETTLED IN WITH MARCO AT ONE OF THE KHAN'S PALACES.

WHAT **SPLENDOR!** WHAT LUXURY!

INDEED! THE EMPEROR DOESN'T HOLD BACK FROM SPENDING FOR HIS RESIDENCE! AND YOU HAVEN'T SEEN THE GARDENS YET!

BUT YOU MUST'VE SEEN SO MANY INCREDIBLE THINGS DURING YOUR TRAVELS. RIGHT, MARCO?

YES, IT'S TRUE! I'VE TRAVELED THROUGHOUT THE WHOLE EMPIRE AND HAVE SEEN SOME WONDERFUL THINGS!

WE'RE REALLY **CURIOUS** TO HEAR YOUR TALES. RIGHT, RATONZO?

WELL... BY AND LARGE...

MY TALES? ACTUALLY, THEY MIGHT BE VERY INTERESTING FOR WESTERNERS!

OUCH!

BAM!

WHAT DID YOU DO TO REMEMBER EVERYTHING? DID YOU KEEP A DIARY PERHAPS?

OF COURSE I WROTE DOWN EVERYTHING I SAW AND EVERY EXCITING THING I EXPERIENCED!

FANTASTIC PLACES, NAMES NEVER HEARD BEFORE, INFORMATION ON THE LIVES OF OTHER PEOPLE... BASICALLY THE LAST 20 YEARS OF MY LIFE!

AND DO YOU HAVE YOUR DIARY HERE WITH YOU? I WOULD VERY MUCH IN FACT, *VERY, VERY MUCH* LIKE TO READ IT!

WELL... YES... I NEVER PART WITH IT!

MAYBE I'LL READ TO YOU FROM IT LATER! BUT NOW, I BET YOU CAN'T WAIT TO VISIT THE CITY!

OF COURSE! WE CAME WITH YOU FOR JUST THAT REASON!

I'D HAVE PREFERRED FORTY WINKS!

YOU DON'T SAY!

THAT EVENING, AFTER A LONG STROLL THROUGH QUINSAI...

PLEASE, GO IN AND GET YOURSELVES SETTLED.

WHILE YOU'RE HERE, I'LL GET MY DIARY SO YOU CAN LEAF THROUGH IT!

HERE IT IS!

HMMM... IT'S VERY *HEAVY!*

SLAM

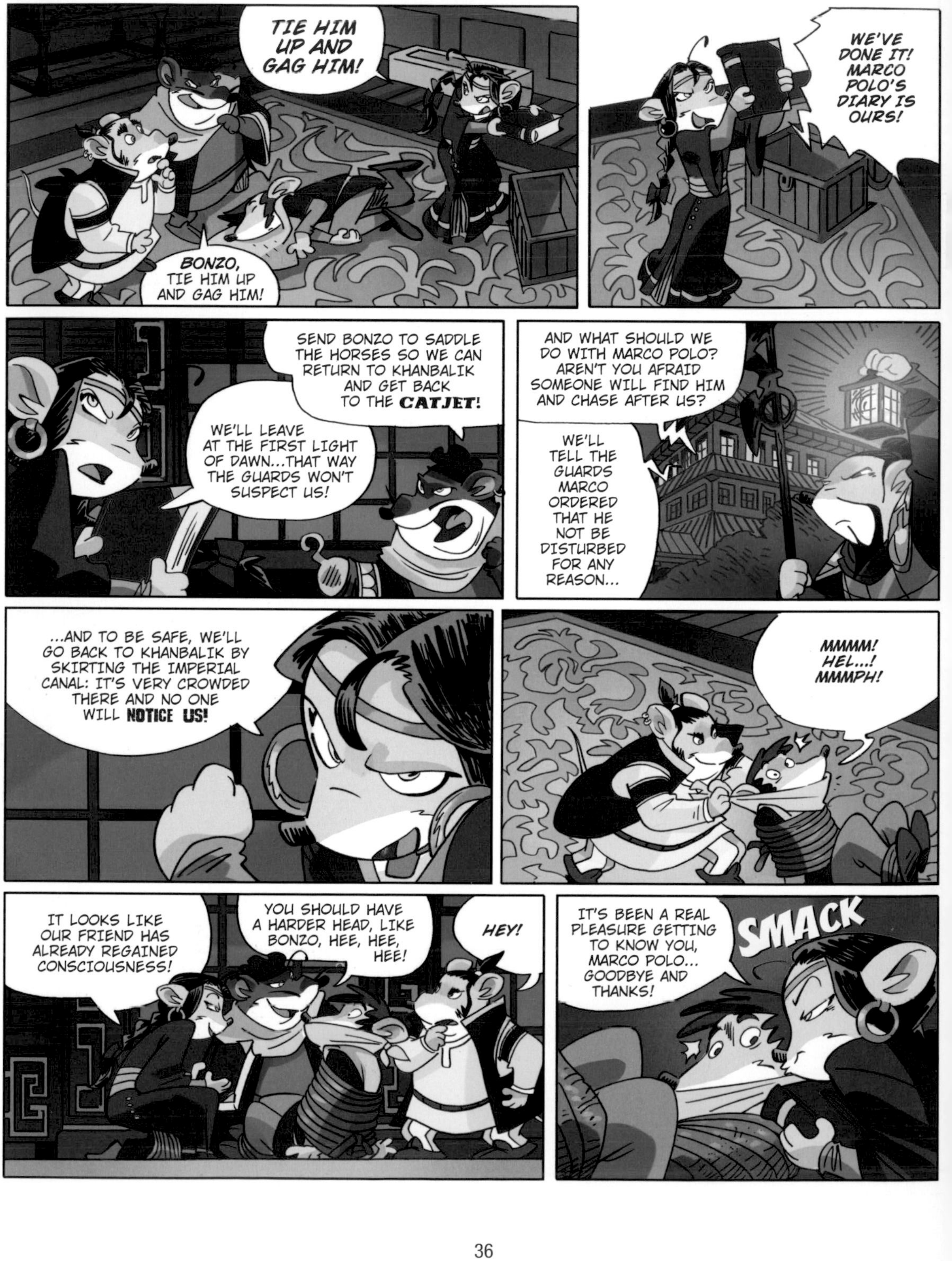

TIE HIM UP AND GAG HIM!
BONZO, TIE HIM UP AND GAG HIM!
WE'VE DONE IT! MARCO POLO'S DIARY IS OURS!
SEND BONZO TO SADDLE THE HORSES SO WE CAN RETURN TO KHANBALIK AND GET BACK TO THE CATJET!
WE'LL LEAVE AT THE FIRST LIGHT OF DAWN...THAT WAY THE GUARDS WON'T SUSPECT US!
AND WHAT SHOULD WE DO WITH MARCO POLO? AREN'T YOU AFRAID SOMEONE WILL FIND HIM AND CHASE AFTER US?
WE'LL TELL THE GUARDS MARCO ORDERED THAT HE NOT BE DISTURBED FOR ANY REASON...
...AND TO BE SAFE, WE'LL GO BACK TO KHANBALIK BY SKIRTING THE IMPERIAL CANAL: IT'S VERY CROWDED THERE AND NO ONE WILL NOTICE US!
MMMM! HEL...! MMMPH!
IT LOOKS LIKE OUR FRIEND HAS ALREADY REGAINED CONSCIOUSNESS!
YOU SHOULD HAVE A HARDER HEAD, LIKE BONZO, HEE, HEE, HEE!
HEY!
IT'S BEEN A REAL PLEASURE GETTING TO KNOW YOU, MARCO POLO... GOODBYE AND THANKS!
SMACK

THE NEXT DAY AT DAWN, MY FRIENDS AND I ARRIVED AT QUINSAI...

HERE IT IS! WE'VE REACHED THE PALACE WHERE MARCO POLO IS STAYING!

BRR... THOSE GUARDS LOOK VERY THREATENING!

GOOD MORNING, MY NAME IS MOUSE-CHECHUNG AND I AM AN OFFICIAL TO HIS MAJESTY THE KHAN! MY FRIENDS AND I WOULD LIKE TO SEE MR. MARCO POLO!

I'M SORRY, BUT MARCO POLO ORDERED THAT HE NOT BE DISTURBED!

BUT I'M A CLOSE FRIEND!

AND WE WERE GIVEN AN ORDER! IS THAT CLEEEEAR?

TSK! WHAT RUDE GUARDS!

IS THERE A PROBLEM, MOUSE-CHECHUNG?

37

UMM...IT SEEMS THAT NO ONE IS ALLOWED TO MEET WITH MARCO POLO FOR THE TIME BEING!

BUT WE *HAVE* TO SEE HIM! IT'S VERY IMPORTANT!

AH...AND HOW COME?

THE TRUTH IS, WE'RE AFRAID THAT MARCO POLO MAY BE IN GRAVE *DANGER!*

IN DANGER?

A BIT UNCOMFORTABLE WITH THE IDEA OF LYING, WE MADE UP A STORY TO JUSTIFY OUR SUSPICIONS...

WHEN WE ARRIVED IN CHINA, WE MET A MERCHANT WHO HAD TRAVELED ALONG THE SILK ROAD: HE TOLD US ABOUT HAVING MET THREE **CATS**...

...WHO BRAGGED TO HIM, SAYING THEY WERE GOING TO BE INTRODUCED AT THE COURT OF THE KHAN, DISGUISED AS MICE!

C-C-CATS???

THE SILK ROAD

WAS A SERIES OF ROUTES THAT CONNECTED CHINA TO THE MIDDLE EAST AND THE MEDITERRANEAN SEA, ALLOWING MERCHANT CARAVANS TO CROSS CENTRAL ASIA. THE MOST COMMONLY TRADED PRODUCTS WERE GOLD, SPICES FOR SEASONING AND PRESERVING FOOD (PEPPER AND NUTMEG) AND VALUABLE CLOTH, INCLUDING SILK WHICH THE ROAD GOT ITS NAME FROM.

RIGHT! WE SUSPECT THEY'RE ACTUALLY THE THREE VENETIAN RODENTS WHO WENT WITH MARCO POLO!

BUT THEN WE HAVE TO WARN MARCO IMMEDIATELY!

IF ONLY THE GUARDS WEREN'T BLOCKING THE DOOR...

THE ONLY SOLUTION IS TO ENTER THE PALACE SECRETLY!

BUT HOW? THE *WALL* IS VERY HIGH!

UMM...

MAYBE YOU COULD TRY TO CLIMB UP AND JUMP OVER THE WALL!

M-ME? YOU KNOW I'M AFRAID OF HEIGHTS!

I'VE GOT A SOLUTION!

?!?

WOW! A CATAPULT!

HUH? A CATAPULT?!?

DO YOU MIND TELLING ME WHERE YOU MANAGED TO FIND IT?

I GOT IT FROM THOSE CRAFTS- MEN OVER THERE!

I TRADED IT FOR THE FRIDGE! THEY DIDN'T UNDER- STAND WHAT IT WAS, BUT THEY'RE USING IT AS AN END TABLE!

YES, BUT WHAT WILL WE DO WITH A CATAPULT? DO YOU WANT TO KNOCK DOWN THE PALACE?

NO, COUSIN! I WAS JUST THINKING OF *FLINGING* YOU OVER THE WALL!

SMAK

HUH?

A LITTLE LATER, BEHIND THE PALACE...

UM... ARE YOU REALLY SURE YOU KNOW WHAT YOU'RE DOING?

>PHEW!< DON'T WORRY, COUSIN! YOU'LL SEE THAT NOTHING'S GOING TO HAPPEN TO YOU! AT LEAST...I HOPE NOT!

CLACK

WOOOSH

OOOPS... I LET GO OF THE ROPE!

SQUEEEEAK!

CRASH

OWOWOWOW! WHY DO I ALWAYS LET MYSELF BE TALKED INTO DOING THESE THINGS?

AT THIS POINT, I JUST HOPE I CAN FIND MARCO POLO BEFORE THE GUARDS FIND ME! HMM, THIS PALACE IS TRULY ENORMOUS...

I'LL TRY LOOKING IN THIS ROOM... UM, EXCUSE ME...IS ANYBODY HERE?

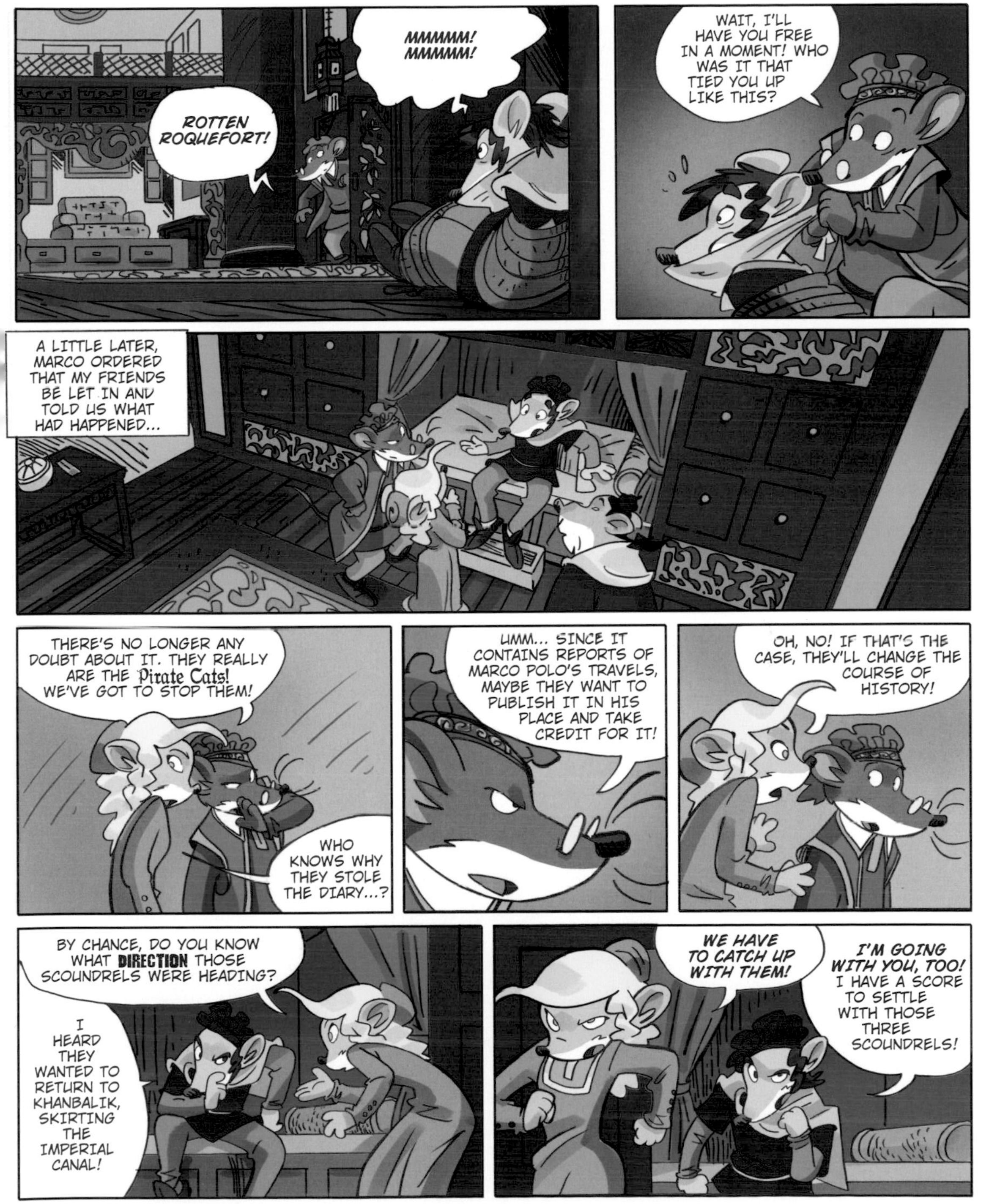
MMMMM! MMMMM!
ROTTEN ROQUEFORT!
WAIT, I'LL HAVE YOU FREE IN A MOMENT! WHO WAS IT THAT TIED YOU UP LIKE THIS?
A LITTLE LATER, MARCO ORDERED THAT MY FRIENDS BE LET IN AND TOLD US WHAT HAD HAPPENED...
THERE'S NO LONGER ANY DOUBT ABOUT IT. THEY REALLY ARE THE Pirate Cats! WE'VE GOT TO STOP THEM!
WHO KNOWS WHY THEY STOLE THE DIARY...?
UMM... SINCE IT CONTAINS REPORTS OF MARCO POLO'S TRAVELS, MAYBE THEY WANT TO PUBLISH IT IN HIS PLACE AND TAKE CREDIT FOR IT!
OH, NO! IF THAT'S THE CASE, THEY'LL CHANGE THE COURSE OF HISTORY!
BY CHANCE, DO YOU KNOW WHAT DIRECTION THOSE SCOUNDRELS WERE HEADING?
I HEARD THEY WANTED TO RETURN TO KHANBALIK, SKIRTING THE IMPERIAL CANAL!
WE HAVE TO CATCH UP WITH THEM!
I'M GOING WITH YOU, TOO! I HAVE A SCORE TO SETTLE WITH THOSE THREE SCOUNDRELS!

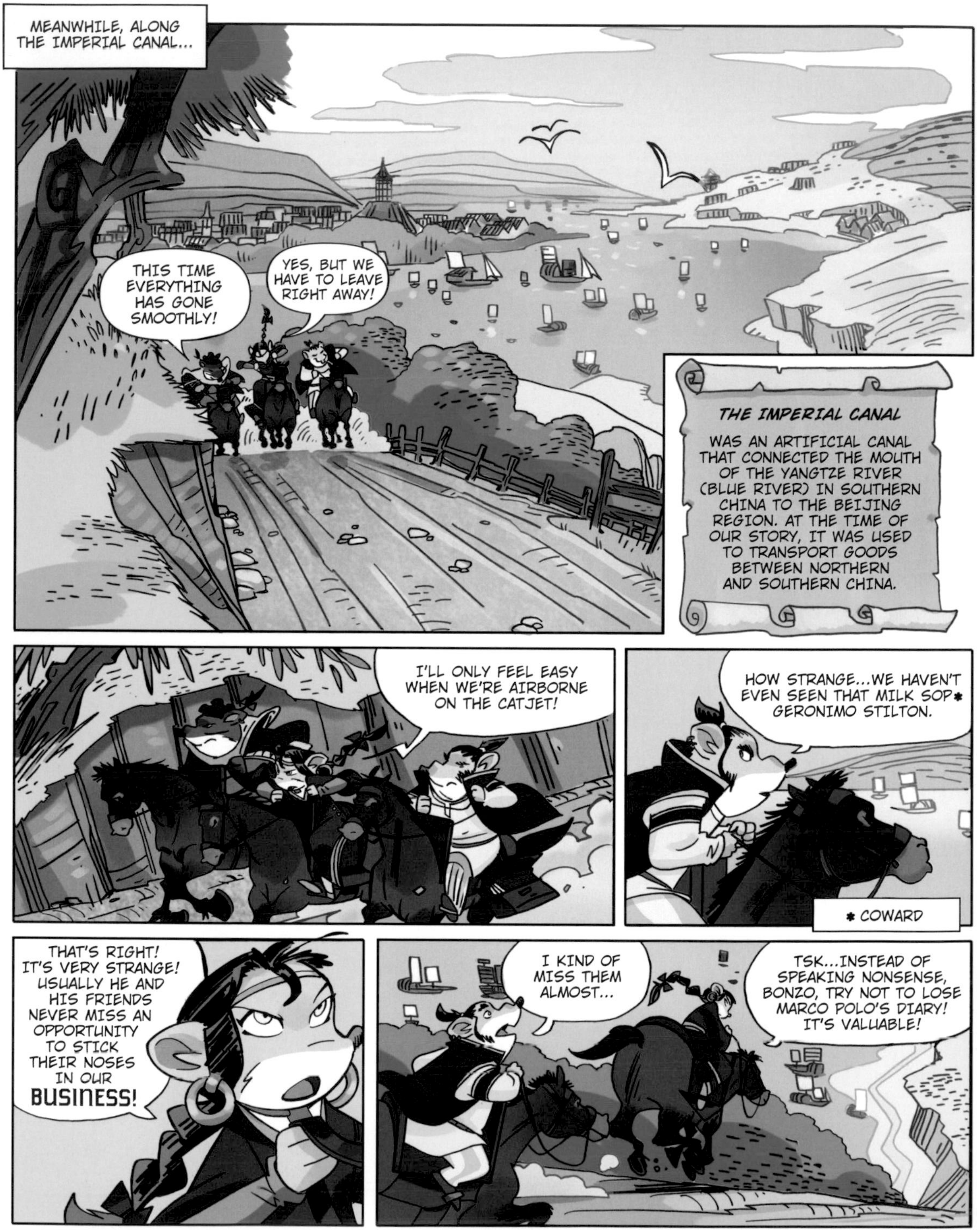
MEANWHILE, ALONG THE IMPERIAL CANAL...
THIS TIME EVERYTHING HAS GONE SMOOTHLY!
YES, BUT WE HAVE TO LEAVE RIGHT AWAY!
THE IMPERIAL CANAL
WAS AN ARTIFICIAL CANAL THAT CONNECTED THE MOUTH OF THE YANGTZE RIVER (BLUE RIVER) IN SOUTHERN CHINA TO THE BEIJING REGION. AT THE TIME OF OUR STORY, IT WAS USED TO TRANSPORT GOODS BETWEEN NORTHERN AND SOUTHERN CHINA.
I'LL ONLY FEEL EASY WHEN WE'RE AIRBORNE ON THE CATJET!
HOW STRANGE...WE HAVEN'T EVEN SEEN THAT MILK SOP* GERONIMO STILTON.
* COWARD
THAT'S RIGHT! IT'S VERY STRANGE! USUALLY HE AND HIS FRIENDS NEVER MISS AN OPPORTUNITY TO STICK THEIR NOSES IN OUR BUSINESS!
I KIND OF MISS THEM ALMOST...
TSK...INSTEAD OF SPEAKING NONSENSE, BONZO, TRY NOT TO LOSE MARCO POLO'S DIARY! IT'S VALUABLE!

DON'T WORRY, TERSILLA, I'M HOLDING IT TIGHTLY IN MY PAWS. **HERE IT IS!**

SWISH

THE DIARY! THE DIARY! WHERE IS IT?

A THOUSAND TUMBLING TABBY CATS! THAT EAGLE TOOK IT! HURRY UP, LET'S CATCH IT!

WRUSH

IT FELL INTO THAT BUSH! I'LL RUN AND GET IT!

UH-OH! YOU AGAIN?!?

GRRR!

NOW WHAT'S GOING ON? IT SEEMS LIKE HORSES ARE **APPROACHING...**

CLOMP CLOMP CLOMP CLOMP CLOMP

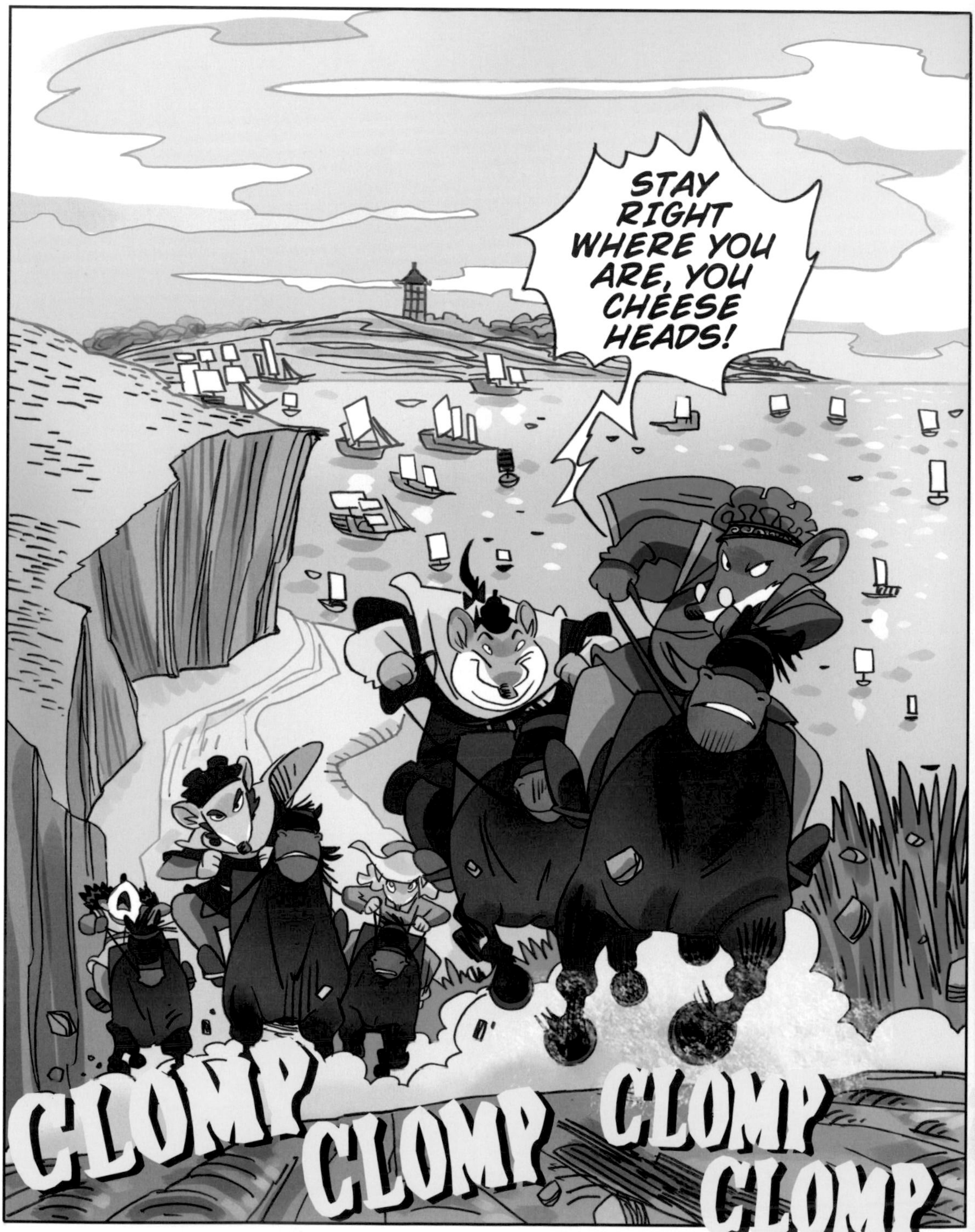
STAY RIGHT WHERE YOU ARE, YOU CHEESE HEADS!
CLOMP
CLOMP
CLOMP
CLOMP

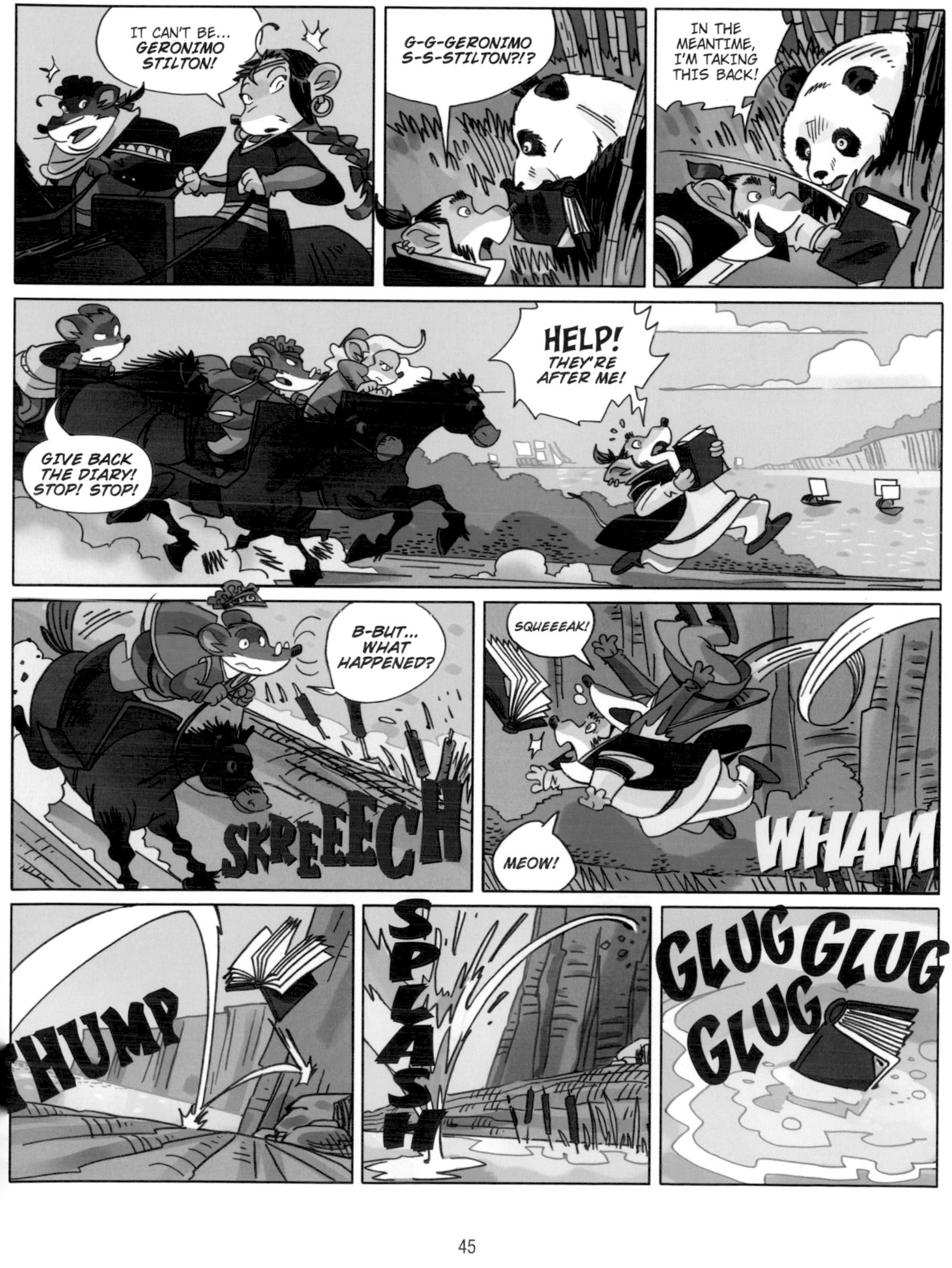
IT CAN'T BE... GERONIMO STILTON!
G-G-GERONIMO S-S-STILTON?!?
IN THE MEANTIME, I'M TAKING THIS BACK!
HELP! THEY'RE AFTER ME!
GIVE BACK THE DIARY! STOP! STOP!
B-BUT... WHAT HAPPENED?
SKREEECH
SQUEEEEAK!
MEOW!
WHAM
THUMP
SPLASH
GLUG GLUG GLUG

MY DIARY! IT WOUND UP IN THE **WATER!**

A THOUSAND TUMBLING TABBY CATS! WE ABSOLUTELY HAVE TO GET IT BACK!

I THINK WE'VE GOT A BIG PROBLEM!

BONZO, DON'T JUST STAND THERE LIKE A STICK! WE HAVE TO GET AWAY! **COME ON!**

>GULP!<

YES, YES... I'M COMING! WAIT FOR ME!

QUICK! WE CAN'T LET THEM TAKE US! HIYAH!

ENJOY YOUR VICTORY, RATS-IN-MY-BOOTS! BUT YOU WON'T BE ABLE TO STOP US NEXT TIME!

NOW WHAT DO WE DO-- FOLLOW THEM?

IT'S USELESS! THEIR PLAN HAS FIZZLED OUT, LUCKILY!

UM...I'M SO SORRY, MARCO!

CHIN UP, MARCO! AT LEAST WE MANAGED TO GET YOU OUT OF THEIR CLUTCHES!

SO WE'VE COME TO THE END OF OUR ADVENTURE: ONCE AGAIN WE FOILED THE PIRATE CATS' PLAN!

DO I HAVE TO SAY IT TO YOU, BONZO?

YES, TERSILLA, I KNOW... IT'S ALL MY FAULT!

WE WERE ALL UPSET THAT MARCO'S DIARY HAD BEEN LOST AND SPOKE LITTLE DURING OUR RETURN...

I DON'T UNDERSTAND, UNCLE GERONIMO: HOW CAN MARCO POLO *WRITE* HIS TRAVELS WITHOUT THE DIARY?

IT WON'T BE A PROBLEM. HE'LL MANAGE TO DO IT ANYWAY!

ACTUALLY, MARCO POLO DIDN'T HAVE ANY DIARY WITH HIM WHEN HE RETURNED FROM CHINA, BUT THANKS TO HIS EXCEPTIONAL MEMORY, HE MANAGED TO REMEMBER AND DICTATE ALL THE ADVENTURES HE'D EXPERIENCED...

...TO AN ITALIAN POET OF THE PERIOD, WHO THEN WROTE *THE TRAVELS OF MARCO POLO!*

WHAT A RELIEF! THEN EVERYTHING'S OKAY!

THE TRAVELS OF MARCO POLO WAS WRITTEN IN 1298, WHILE MARCO WAS A PRISONER OF THE CITY OF GENOA. IT WAS NOT MARCO WHO WROTE THE BOOK, BUT ONE OF HIS FELLOW CELL MATES, RUSTICELLO DA PISA, WHO MARCO TOLD ABOUT HIS ADVENTURES. IN 1299, MARCO WAS SET FREE AND RETURNED TO VENICE; THE BOOK WAS PUBLISHED IN OLD FRENCH. LATER ON, IT WAS CALLED IL MILIONE, PERHAPS DUE TO THE NAME "EMILIONE," IN REMEMBRANCE OF AN ANCESTOR IN THE POLO FAMILY WHO WAS CALLED THAT.

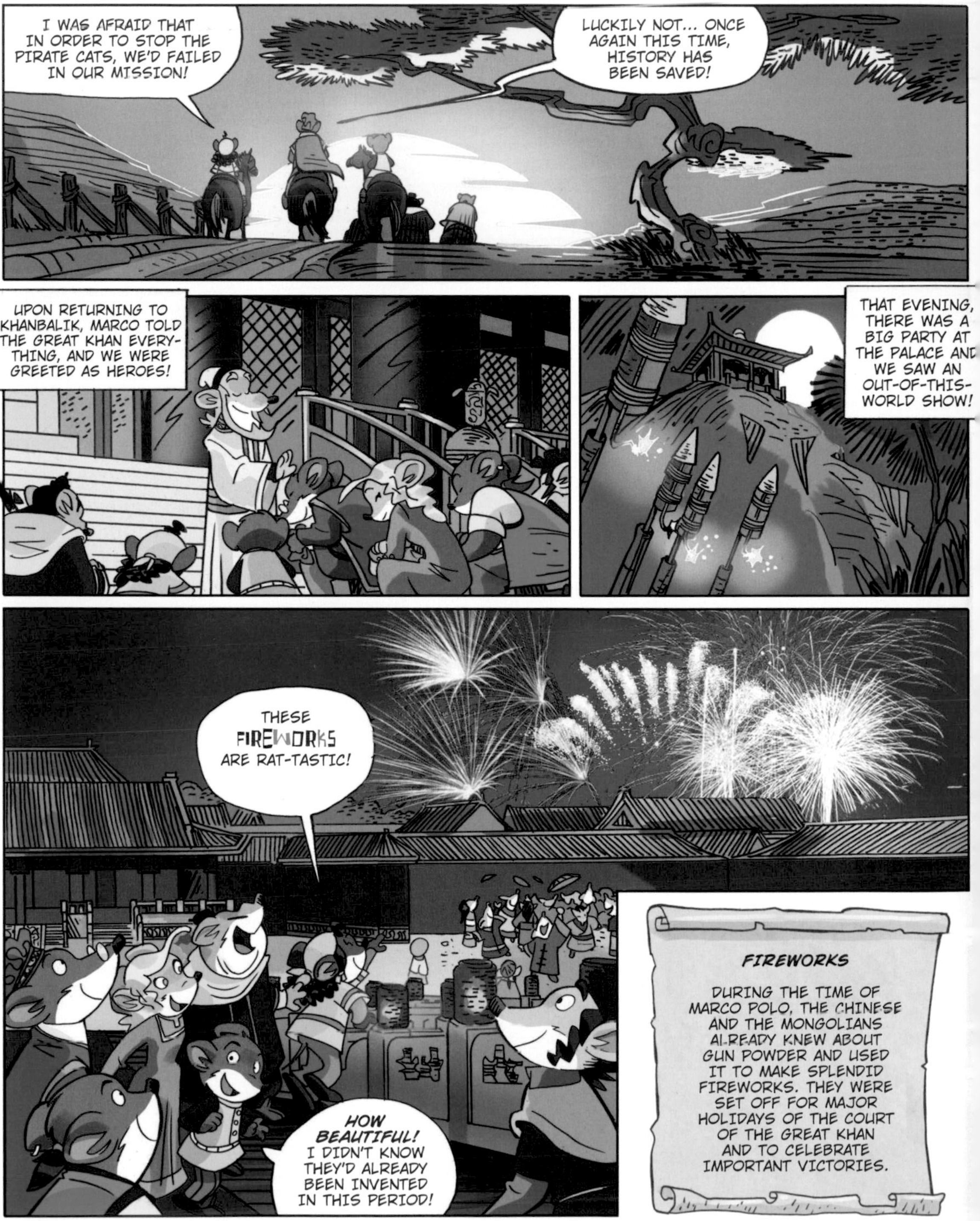
I WAS AFRAID THAT IN ORDER TO STOP THE PIRATE CATS, WE'D FAILED IN OUR MISSION!
LUCKILY NOT... ONCE AGAIN THIS TIME, HISTORY HAS BEEN SAVED!
UPON RETURNING TO KHANBALIK, MARCO TOLD THE GREAT KHAN EVERY-THING, AND WE WERE GREETED AS HEROES!
THAT EVENING, THERE WAS A BIG PARTY AT THE PALACE AND WE SAW AN OUT-OF-THIS-WORLD SHOW!
THESE FIREWORKS ARE RAT-TASTIC!
HOW BEAUTIFUL! I DIDN'T KNOW THEY'D ALREADY BEEN INVENTED IN THIS PERIOD!
FIREWORKS
DURING THE TIME OF MARCO POLO, THE CHINESE AND THE MONGOLIANS ALREADY KNEW ABOUT GUN POWDER AND USED IT TO MAKE SPLENDID FIREWORKS. THEY WERE SET OFF FOR MAJOR HOLIDAYS OF THE COURT OF THE GREAT KHAN AND TO CELEBRATE IMPORTANT VICTORIES.

THE NEXT DAY, WE SAID GOODBYE TO OUR FRIENDS AND RETURNED TO THE SPEEDRAT!

JUST AS THE POLOS HAD MISSED VENICE, WE, TOO, HAD REALLY MISSED OUR HOME! SO WE FINALLY ARRIVED AT PROFESSOR VON VOLT'S LAB...

FRIENDS! YOU'RE FINALLY HERE AGAIN! WELCOME BACK!

PROFESSOR VON VOLT! IT'S GREAT TO SEE YOU AGAIN!

FROM YOUR SMILES, I GATHER THAT THE MISSION WAS A SUCCESS, RIGHT?

YES, INDEED...

THE PIRATE CATS WANTED TO STEAL MARCO POLO'S DIARY AND PUBLISH IT IN HIS PLACE, BUT WE MANAGED TO FOIL THEIR **TREACHEROUS** PLAN!

DID THEY ACTUALLY WANT TO DO SOMETHING LIKE THAT? THOSE CATS REALLY ARE **SCOUNDRELS!**

TELL ME ALL THE DETAILS LATER! BUT NOW LET'S SIT DOWN AND HAVE SOMETHING TO EAT... I IMAGINE THE JOURNEY MADE YOU HUNGRY!

I'M AS HUNGRY AS A CAT!

I'M GLAD TO SEE THAT YOUR COUSIN DIGESTED MY EARPHONES COMPLETELY!

UM...THAT'S RIGHT!

ANYHOW, WHILE YOU WERE AWAY, I ALREADY TOOK CARE OF MAKING MORE SPARES!

AND WHERE DID YOU PUT THEM, PROFESSOR?

WHERE? WELL, I PUT THEM ON...

OH, NO! HE ATE THEM AGAIN!

>BURP!<

HA, HA, HA, HA, HA, HA!

MY DEAR RODENT FRIENDS, FAREWELL UNTIL THE NEXT ADVENTURE... ANOTHER WHISKERFUL OF AN ADVENTURE, WRITTEN BY STILTON...
Geronimo Stilton!

Watch Out For PAPERCUTZ

Welcome to the fantastic, Far East-filled, fourth GERONIMO STILTON graphic novel from Papercutz, the folks dedicated to publishing great graphic novels for all ages. You may wonder how did little ol' Papercutz wind up publishing the exciting adventures of such a world-famouse journalist? Well, it all began during a meeting in Manhattan, in the palatial Papercutz offices, during a meeting with my publishing partner Terry Nantier and we were talking about what would be a sensational addition to our stellar line-up—Excuse me, I forgot to introduce myself. My name is Salicrup, *Jim Salicrup*, and I'm the Editor-in-Chief at Papercutz. Terry mentioned that he had seen samples of the Italian GERONIMO STILTON graphic novels on one of his business trips overseas, and suggested that Papercutz publish these graphic novels in English. Since Terry knows more about graphic novels than anyone else I know—he's a true pioneer in the field and is responsible for bringing much of Europe's finest comics to an appreciative American audience—I simply nodded in agreement and the rest is history!

GERONIMO STILTON has become one of our most successful titles at Papercutz, and the reviews have been positively glowing! But it occurs to me that some GERONIMO STILTON fans may not be aware of the many other graphic novel series also published by Papercutz. When I mentioned that to Terry, he exclaimed "**MOLDY MOZZARELLA!** You better fix that with your next 'Watch Out for Papercutz' editorial—OR ELSE!" Well, when Terry squeaks, er, I mean speaks, I listen! So without further ado, here are just a few of the latest and greatest Papercutz graphic novels you may find irresistible...

If you love adventure, the LEGO® NINJAGO graphic novels pack in page-after-page of non-stop action! Each volume features all-new stories starring Cole, Zane, Jay, and Kai, the Masters of Spinjitzu, by Greg Farshtey, and artists such as Paulo Henrique, Paul Lee, and Jolyon Yates.

Equally action-packed is SABAN'S POWER RANGERS SUPER SAMURAI, starring the longest-running TV super-heroes The Red Ranger, The Pink Ranger, The Blue Ranger, The Green Ranger, The Yellow Ranger, and, of course, The Gold Ranger, in all-new adventures written by Stefan Petrucha, and illustrated by Paulo Henrique.

If silly slapstick is more your speed you'll love our all-new graphic novels starring THE THREE STOOGES, featuring screwball stories starring Moe, Larry, and Curly, by George Gladir and Stefan Petrucha, and drawn by award-winning cartoonist Stan Goldberg. There's also the crazy companion series, THE BEST OF THE THREE STOOGES COMICBOOKS featuring classic comics by Norman Maurer and Pete Alvarado.

I could go on, but instead I'll simply suggest you check out our wondrous website at www.papercutz.com to get all the latest news and information on the full line of graphic novels Papercutz has to offer. Just as Geronimo Stilton loves to talk about his awesome adventures through time to thwart the evil plans of the Pirate Cats, I'd love to tell you about such Papercutz graphic novels as THE SMURFS and CLASSICS ILLUSTRATED, but I don't want you to think I'm trying to sell you something! So, until next time, keep an eye out for pussy-cats wearing mouse masks, chances are they may be up to no good!

Thanks,

Jim

Caricature of Jim by Steve Brodner at the MoCCA Art Fest.

Don't miss GERONIMO STILTON Graphic Novel #5 – "The Great Ice Age"

The Great Ice Age

IT WAS A PEACEFUL **SUNNY** MORNING AND I FOUND MYSELF AT THE NEW MOUSE CITY GOLF COURSE...

...WITH MY NEPHEW BENJAMIN, MY FRIEND PETUNIA, AND HER DAUGHTER BUGSY.

EXCUSE ME, I HAVEN'T INTRODUCED MYSELF YET: MY NAME IS STILTON, *Geronimo Stilton!* AND I EDIT THE RODENT'S GAZETTE, THE MOST FAMOUS PAPER ON MOUSE ISLAND!

SIOK

SSSSSS

DON'T BOTHER TAKING IT, GERONIMO. YOU CAN SEE THE NEXT SHOT WILL BE BETTER!

YOU'RE SO NICE, PETUNIA!

YOU KNOW, I'VE WANTED TO SPEND A BIT OF TIME WITH YOU FOR SO LONG...

...WELL, HERE...WHAT I WANT TO SAY IS THAT WHEN WE'RE TOGETHER, I...

WAKE UP, GRANDSON!!!!

SQUEEEEAK!

GRANDPA WILLIAM?!? WHAT ARE YOU DOING HERE?

I'M PLAYING WITH MY FRIEND, LONGSHOT PUTTER, DIRECTOR OF THE NEW MOUSE CITY SUBWAY!

GOOD MORNING!

BUT YOU, HOWEVER, WHY AREN'T YOU AT WORK?

WELL, HERE'S...

WHEN I RAN THE PAPER, I WOULD NEVER HAVE DREAMED OF TAKING A DAY OFF, NEVER!

BUT GRANDPA, TODAY'S SUNDAY, SO I THOUGHT I'D...

I KNOW PERFECTLY WELL WHAT DAY IT IS, JUST LIKE I KNOW PERFECTLY WELL THAT YOU'RE A LAZYPAWS!

ENJOY YOUR GAME, BUT I WANT AN ARTICLE ON GOLF TOMORROW!

>SIGH!< I'VE GOT A FEELING I'M DONE RELAXING FOR TODAY!

WHEN GRANDPA WILLIAM HAD GONE AWAY...

WONDERFUL SHOT, UNCLE!

THE BALL **SOARED AWAY** AS FAR AS THE EYE CAN SEE!

A LITTLE TOO FAR! I'M NOT SURE I KNOW WHICH DIRECTION IT WENT!

SQUEEEAK!

OOPS! SORRY, COUSIN, I GAUGED THE TRAJECTORY OF MY SHOT BADLY!

TRAP!?!

I DIDN'T KNOW YOU LIKED TO PLAY GOLF!

I DON'T JUST LIKE IT: I'M A CHAMPION!

THE SECRET TO GOLF IS TO PLACE THE BALL ON THE GROUND WELL...

...AND THEN HIT IT WITH ALL THE POWER YOU'VE GOT!

SWNTSSSHH

SPLAFF

GERONIMO, ARE YOU OKAY?

UM...YES...

SEE, COUSIN? I'M A REAL CHAMPION!

Don't miss GERONIMO STILTON Graphic Novel #5 – "The Great Ice Age"

56